CLIMBING THE MAST

A Collection of Short Stories and Poems

by Bridget Arregger

Copyright © Bridget Arregger
All rights reserved *2015*

The moral rights of the author have been asserted

Climbing the Mast

ISBN 978-1-326-14989-5
Published by AudioArcadia.com 2015

This book, which includes text and cover artwork, is sold on the condition that it is not lent, resold, hired out, performed, recorded, distributed, circulated or handed out by any other method to any other party, including third parties, agents, retailers or any other source of distribution without the prior consent of the publisher. The publisher can be contacted by email at info@audioarcadia.com

ACKNOWLEDGEMENTS

The Duck and Thistle - One of four winning stories chosen for Audio Arcadia's Short Stories, Volume One – available from www.audioarcadia.com

Dust - http://flashfloodjournal.blogspot.co.uk

Autumn Wishes - shortlisted for Writing Magazine Annual Competition, read on Corinium Radio and printed in Somewhere Else Writers' anthology 2013.

J.E.E - read on Corinium Radio 2013.

Flirtatious Foodie in Harrods - printed in Somewhere Else anthology 2013.

Eve Bites First - second place in Yeovil Literary Prize, printed in Graffiti, the magazine of Writers in the Brewery, Cirencester 2012.

Things to do Every Day - poem, Graffiti 2012

Sail With Me - A Somonka - Graffiti 2011

REVIEWS

'Bridget's story *Dust* demands to be re-read. Wonderfully subtle and sinister. I'll never look at a duster the same way again. And certainly never use one.' - *John Holland, Stroud Short Stories.*

'Bridget has an extraordinary imagination and an ability to lure the reader gently into her strange and often troubling worlds.' - *Sophie Livingston, Somewhere Else Writers.*

'This collection of short stories explores both the drama inherent in everyday life and the magical, fantastical realms of science fiction. We hear from a child lost on the moon, from a contemporary of Jesus, and see Adam through Eve's eyes. From the dangers of online dating to the spooky mobility of kelp, these stories will entertain, amuse and stir the reader's emotions.' - *Kim Fleet.*

'Bridget Arregger is an original and accomplished writer of short stories with a strong individual voice.' - *Bea Davenport,* author of *In Too Deep, This Little Piggy* and *The Serpent House.*

CONTENTS

	Page
Ups and Downs	5
Seven of Hearts	8
Kelp	14
A Flirtatious Foodie in Harrods	17
Climbing the Mast	18
Parallel Magnolias	23
Why I Don't Go Jogging Any More	28
J.E.E.	29
Tripos	33
Eve Bites First	39
Baby Shoes	42
Things To Do Every Day	43
No Milk Today	44
I Left My Womb in Chaguaramus	46
Autumn Wishes	52
Dust	57
Gospel According to an Unknown Friend	59
An Aggressive Surgeon in Windsor Castle	61
The Duck and Thistle	63
Good Neighbour	72
Lost on the Moon	75
Sisters	80
The Yellow Hat	81
Sail With Me	83
Criss-Cross	84
Which Diagnosis? or *Clarity Begins At Home*	90

UPS AND DOWNS

'I do wish you were feeling a bit more cuddly this morning,' he said in what might be mistaken for plaintive tones.

She put aside the Sunday paper and gazed irritably at the top of his head, noting the dandruff flecking the edges of his thinning patch and warm familiar smell of unwashed hair. Faint feelings of aversion began to percolate through her body.

'I'm sorry,' she offered, but sharply: more a reprimand than an apology. He said nothing, his hunched back seemingly intended as sufficient rebuke.

He had put his pillow over her tummy, complaining that it was too noisy in there for closer comfort and was snuggled down on her lap while she sat propped against the protesting headboard.

A warm sweaty hand began exploring the folds in her nightdress. His touch succeeded in increasing her revulsion. She tried to be sociable.

'I was just thinking about how we could use up that cooked chicken. Any ideas?'

Heaving inwardly at the thought of cold greasy chicken, she resisted the desire to push him violently away, gently detached his fingers, slid out of bed and plodded downstairs.

'Hormones!' she muttered ruefully as she stumbled about in the kitchen, catching her hip on the corner of a cupboard that had wandered inconsiderately into her path.

'I wonder,' she said aloud, as she switched on the kettle, put a teaspoonful of tea into each mug and carefully measured milk and sugar into the teapot, 'I wonder, after the menopause, when my ovaries have stopped pumping vast quantities of oestrogen, or progesterone, or whatever, around my body at regular intervals, shall I have all good days or all bad days?'

'I wonder,' she repeated, as she washed out the mugs and teapot and tried again, 'will I be caught up on a magnificent wave of physical ecstasy, revelling in unending sexual play, gourmet food and energetic sports? Will I become a brilliantly articulate raconteur?

'More likely,' she sighed, as she mopped up the floor and refilled the kettle, 'more likely, I will be permanently reduced to this clumsy bunch of jangled nerves, stuttering and gibbering incomprehensively.'

'Or perhaps,' she said, as this time the boiling water poured itself uneventfully into the teapot, 'perhaps I won't have either good days or bad days. Perhaps all the emotion will go out of my life: the love and the hurt, the heights of passion and the depths of ineptitude, levelling out into a constant state of calm acquiescence. Will that leave me as a serene earth mother or a boring worn-out drudge?'

She switched on the radio and listened with growing interest as the presenter tripped and stuttered her way through a series of routine announcements.

'Hah!' she said, 'I bet your period is due in a couple of days too. What would you say if I phoned in and asked you?'

Brrr . . .Brrr . . . 'Good morning, is that so and so? Would you mind terribly telling me if you're due to come on, to menstruate, tomorrow? You see I couldn't help noticing you were having trouble with your lines just now. And I've got this theory, you see, based on my own experience, about women not being able to find the right words to say what they're trying to explain when it's just before their period and I thought perhaps you were one of them if you see what I mean and, well, are you?'

'Actually no, but I suppose I was rather preoccupied, having had too much to drink and wondering what to do with a whole lot of chicken left over from a party last night and I'm hung-over and my husband has walked out, my children have left home, and, if you really want to know, I'm sixty-two and I had a total hysterectomy and both ovaries removed two years ago. I wish I were only suffering pre-menstrual stress. I can't even use it as an excuse. Sorry I can't help you.'

'Um, well, I see, sorry to have bothered you.'

No, she wouldn't phone, it wouldn't be right, and besides, she might be put through to the wrong person and be given some most peculiar answers. The presenter had sounded so young. Just shows how difficult it is to judge when you can't think straight.

Giggling to herself, she arranged a tray and carried it cautiously upstairs.

He had fallen asleep; his tousled hair flopped carelessly on the itinerant pillow. Abandoning the tray, she bent down and kissed him. He didn't smell so bad really.

'Give me a couple of days,' she whispered, as she curled up beside him.

'I don't want you today, but you know what I'm like when I'm in the mood.'

And they snatched a few more moments of peace together before their children woke.

SEVEN OF HEARTS

Roger hated Saturday afternoons to be fine and sunny. He especially hated them to be blustery, cold and sunny, like today. He would have to think of something to do with the children. Sheila insisted he take them out. Out of doors. He was not an outdoorsy sort of person. Neither were they. Mike had to be dragged away from the computer, Sonia from her mathematical puzzles. Fresh air was alien.

They had a system for Saturday afternoons. Roger fetched the cards and spread them in a fan. Sonia selected the first one. Three of Spades. The beach. Far too cold. Even Sheila would not expect the beach today. Spades stood for the beach, the garden or the allotment. By some unfortunate accident, most of the spades were just-perceptibly dog-eared. This pack had been withdrawn from general use. Michael took a card. Two of diamonds. Kite-flying. What a pity it was actually too windy. They all agreed on that. Kites had their moments, once you have been dragged out, but it was a long way up the hill to the best spot. Apart from the deuce, diamonds signified rainy days, sparkling drops of rain, gems in the geological museum. It was a simple system. Roger's turn. Jack of Clubs. Walk. They all groaned. The King of Clubs would have been good - crazy golf. The Queen - real golf. They were allowed to ignore the Queen as they were marched around the golf course at intervals by Sheila and she did not want them to learn bad habits under Roger's supervision. They pretended they had not seen the Jack.

Sonia again. Seven of Hearts. Hearts were healthy: ten for tennis, eight for rowing and so on. Tennis was altogether too ghastly to contemplate. Such a shame that card was torn slightly. Seven for swimming - after the Seven Swans. Now that was a possibility. Even the train ride to the pool in the next town was acceptable.

Sheila had fewer spies in the next town and that pool was for sliding, not real swimming. The indoor pool was not outdoors, it is true, but it was a proper activity. They were supposed to keep the swimming pool for rainy days but they might get away with it. OK, except that Roger couldn't swim and hated sitting in the chlorine-laden air, waiting, if the rest of the swamp gang did not turn up. He was not permitted to drop the children off. He had forgotten to collect them once and, besides, that wouldn't be spending the afternoon with them.

'Well?'

'OK. We'll swim.' Michael answered for them all.

'If we go now, we can go to the cinema afterwards?' Sonia liked the cinema. This was not allowed on sunny days, but easy to keep quiet about. They would avoid popcorn, which might stick to their clothes. Michael and Roger preferred videos, but it was Sonia's turn to choose.

It was such a waste of an afternoon. Roger regretted not being able to find things they could all enjoy but that was impossible on fine days. Wet days were just about bearable as although they had to leave the house, they could huddle with someone else's computer or video. They had to put in a minimal appearance at museums, but that was not too much of a hardship.

Saturdays were the only time they were allowed to see each other and they were absolutely forbidden to play poker together. Or snooker. Not even in someone else's house. Sheila would know. She would smell the cigarette smoke in their hair, the alcohol on Roger's breath. She could tell from the look in their eyes. It was not worth the effort to disobey. She would get another court order and they wouldn't be able to meet at all.

Roger did not hate Sheila. Just Sheila's ideas about how to bring up the children. Which is why they were divorced. He was looking forward to when the twins were old enough to decide for themselves. Then you'd see. At eight, Mike showed distinct promise as a snooker player. He could be a champion given the right environment. Roger had saved nearly enough to buy the discarded table from Armand. He would have it by their next birthday. It was one of Roger's rules never to buy on credit or to borrow money. He had his vices, but he would never risk becoming indebted to another man or waste money in interest. He played poker for money but did not gamble. He made sure he won. On balance. They would install the snooker table in the garage. The car lived outside anyway. With sufficient care, they would be able to arrange some regular playing. The garage was not in the house, was it?

Sonia was destined to be a mathematician. In the days before the ban, she had played poker well enough with Roger's friends to earn herself some interesting pocket money, but it would always remain a hobby. She won too easily, there was insufficient challenge. And she was too curious, too imaginative to remain in a murky underworld like her father.

'Yes, fine. Anything good on? Well, never mind, we'll see when we get there.'

They fetched their swimming things. Sonia insisted that Roger bring his too.

'You never know,' she said with sanguine acceptance, 'you might meet someone.'

'If she can swim, I don't want to know her.'

There were no trains running. They had to take the bus. They rode upstairs in the front. It was a beautiful day. Bright. Sunny. Bushy-tailed. Even Roger had to admit he felt uplifted. The bus route was unfamiliar. They almost missed their stop. As they scrambled off, Roger brushed against a woman getting on. Her hair was wet. She smelled of chlorine. She smiled at Roger. He held her eyes as the bus moved off.

'Maybe you're right,' he said to Sonia.

'What?'

'Never mind.'

Roger changed into his trunks and tucked a pack of cards and a packet of cigarettes into the waistband. The gang played for cigarettes. Roger ought to cut down on his smoking but short of giving them away, what was he to do? He spread his towel over his shoulders and sneaked past the foot trough without getting his feet wet. The children were already in the pool.

There were no other non-swimming parents in the swamp behind the changing rooms yet. Roger started playing patience in a dilatory way.

'We could play snap,' a voice behind him said. Roger swung round. It was the woman from the bus. She was wearing a lightweight racing swim suit, with a track suit top slung around her waist. Her long wet hair hung in heavy strands over her shoulders.

'Hi, how're you?' Roger spoke mechanically, his mind grappling with reality. How had she got here? And why? Had she followed them back to the pool?

'What are you doing here?' The question slipped out of its own accord.

The woman smiled. It was a warm expansive smile, less shy than on the bus.

'I work here. My name's Wendy and I'm a lifeguard. I've seen you here before and don't tell me you've never noticed me.' She adjusted her posture in a way that would be hard not to notice and laughed. 'Hey, don't mind me. Come on, move over. You look as if you could use some company. I've just finished my shift and we should be able to get a game going soon.'

Game? His mind wouldn't work. Lifeguard? That was off the scale. But she was stunning. Was she really interested in him? Forget it. It couldn't last. It would be worse than with Sheila.

Wendy would demand something more athletic than he was capable of.

'Game? What sort of game?' He could not keep the alarm out of his voice.

'Poker. You are one of the gang, aren't you? I'm not mistaking you for someone else?'

'Yes. Er, no.' Relief sent shivers all through his body. 'But I think I must be mistaking you for someone. I've just seen you get on a bus.'

'No wonder you looked phased. I thought . . . No, never mind what I thought. That must have been my sister, Tess. We're very alike. To look at anyway. We're not a bit alike in other ways. She was here earlier. I'm trying to teach her to swim. She hates it, but we agreed she would teach me to play poker and I would teach her to swim. Two of those essentials for survival in this world.'

'I know about swimming and that it might be useful, by the sea, and poker keeps me alive, but what is it to you?'

'So I can win back the housekeeping my husband loses and, with any luck, teach him too. I don't think he realises he's being taken for a ride.'

'Ah. You have a husband?'

'Yes. Oh, I'm sorry, I'm not trying to make a pass, you know. Just being friendly. Well,' she grinned, 'that's not quite honest. My sister said would I try to get to know you so I could introduce you.'

Roger's brain started to function.

'Could you teach me to swim?'

'I could try. Tessy would be tickled.'

'How long would it take for me to catch up with her?'

'Not long.'

'Can we start now?'

Mike and Sonia were astonished to see their father gripping tightly onto their friend Wendy-the-lifeguard's arm, standing chest deep in a quiet corner away from the slides. They winked at each other and wisely affected not to notice. They didn't want to put him off. Although they always pretended not to like anything energetic, they loved the water slides and were always disappointed when he wouldn't join them. They did not know what it felt like not to be able to swim. Sheila had insisted on it, practically from birth.

The first lesson was not a success. Roger would not talk about it. It did not help that the only available films in the town were re-runs of *Jaws* and *The Perfect Storm*. They chose a video after all.

Next Saturday it was pouring with rain. Excellent weather. They didn't bother with the cards. As soon as they arrived, Mike and Sonia fetched their swimming togs from the line in the bathroom where they had hung them out last week. They put their bags by Roger's stuffed hold-all on the kitchen table and couldn't help noticing that the pocket that usually held the cards and cigarettes was hanging open, empty. Roger saw their glances.

'There's a time for everything,' he said, 'I don't want them to get wet'.

KELP

Benjamin was the first to notice that they could move. Like Triffids, he thought, and his first impulse was to run and tell his brother. It was time to go home anyway and his mother would be cross if he was much later, but, fascinated, he stayed and watched for a while.

He and Tom had noticed some time ago that a new kind of seaweed was appearing along the shoreline. Intermingled with the regular kelp, with its broad brown ribbons, stubby stems and tough roots, there were some plants that had developed upright thick stalks with fleshy, scaly tops. As the waves rolled over the fronds, those with the stalks lifted higher than the others and the roots loosened in the sand.

Ben watched as one stem lifted itself out of the sand again so that the roots were exposed and let the water drift it to a new spot where it settled back into the sand. It was a small movement that could have been an accident of a particularly strong current. As Ben watched it became more and more obvious to him that the movements were not accidental but deliberate and the kelp was inching its way towards the shore. It was the sort of event that you wouldn't notice if you weren't specially looking, like limpets swimming away from their rocks to feed and returning when your back is turned.

Ben waded to the line of rocks that lay between the sand bar and the beach. With each new wave, more of the kelp stems lifted clear of the sand and floated nearer to the rocks. Then Ben saw what he was waiting for: a large rooted stem pulled completely out of the sand, appeared to wait for the next wave, and then allowed itself to be wafted up on to the rock. Several other kelp plants followed until there was a small row of stems, waving their bulbous heads, looking like a line of curious young long necked cormorants. Ben watched a moment more then ran to fetch Tom. Tea would have to wait.

Over the next few days, more of the kelp made it up on to the rocks and the biggest one, the leader, reached the beach first. By now all the children from the hamlet gathered each day to watch the kelp progress. Soon, many of the plants had made it on to the beach. Unlike Triffids, the tallest plant was less than forty centimetres high and most of the others were not much more than thirty so they did not seem in the least bit threatening. They moved so slowly, after all, and when the children bent down to peer at them, or touch them, they waved their heads in a benign way, seemingly as curious as the children. One of the children pulled off a broad leafy lamina from one of the smallest specimens, but it just continued to wave its head gently and settled its roots deeper into the sand. The children marked it with a piece of string and next time they looked, found that it had grown several new laminae around the cut, just as a lettuce, or a shrub, or any other plant produces new growth when cut or pruned.

Gradually the adults drifted down to the beach to examine the new arrivals. Naturally, before long, the pragmatists had pulled off fronds, cooked them in the way of other seaweeds, and sampled them. They were surprisingly tasty and soon the whole hamlet was treating itself to the new free food. The kelp continued to replenish itself after harvesting and the numbers reaching the beach increased. There did not seem to be a seasonal fluctuation, no-one got ill or suffered any noticeable ill effects and the new kelp soon became a staple part of the hamlet diet.

Only Granny May was cautious. She had an uncomfortable feeling about the new algae and swore that when she peered into the hidden dark recesses between the petal-like fleshy scales on the heads, a pair of tiny black eyes was staring back at her, in a sad and pleading way. She refused to eat them and took to visiting them on the beach, bending down as if she was talking to the kelp as they gathered around her. Hence, Granny May was the first to see the leader, now marked with one of her bright red ribbons, take its first hesitant steps up the beach without the benefit of the waves.

Before long many of the plants could move about freely on the beach and began to test their roots on the cobble stones of the hamlet. Slowly but surely they began to explore the various gardens and buildings. They wandered freely in and out of the houses, always gently swaying, seemingly curious, and benign. They left no mess, apart from a tiny sprinkling of sand, did not need feeding and made no noise.

Things continued in this manner for several years. The kelp was apparently highly nutritious and everyone seemed healthy and well.

Nevertheless, Granny May was not surprised when Ben's mother mentioned to her how Ben's and Tom's finger nails and toe nails seemed to be softening and going brown, getting worse daily, and to ask if Granny May had any remedy. Granny May examined the offending nails and shook her head sadly. She was not one to say 'I told you so' but in a roundabout way advised Ben's mother to stop feeding her family with the mobile kelp.

Granny May did the best she could for all the villagers but it made no difference. Now, in various places, there are areas with delicious kelp that can move around, apparently curious and benign. And there are those that say if you stare into the dark recesses in their fleshy, scaly heads, you get the feeling that there is a pair of tiny black eyes peering out in a sad and pleading way.

A FLIRTATIOUS FOODIE IN HARRODS

Young man could you please hand me down that tin
of caviar at eighty pounds, the gold
one. Can't quite reach and you're so tall, so thin,
most handsome too if I may be so bold,
my dear, such lovely curls, so rare today,
I find, amongst the young. Most want to shave
their heads, but come, don't run so fast away.
I need some help so please do me a favour; put your mind to helping with my feast.
Some salmon, smoked or fresh, will do, don't you
agree? More elegant than bird or beast.
And what about some truffles, wild, a few
and wine, the most expensive that you stock.
Now hold these while I go to choose my frock.

Author's Note: This was prompted by an exercise in which the words Foodie, Harrods and Flirtatious were drawn from hats and is written in Elizabethan sonnet form.
    There are fourteen lines in Iambic Pentameter, divided into three quatrains and a couplet. The rhyme scheme is abab cdcd efef gg.
    It is best read aloud, for the sense of it rather than the rhymes.

CLIMBING THE MAST

Today, I am going to climb the mast. It is time. I am ready.

I have never had a head for heights: if I had to stand on a chair to change a light bulb, my legs would shake. However, I am getting better; sailing has been good for me. I can climb ladders now and it is not that I have become braver or am less of a wimp: faced with a new horror, I am just as wimpish. Give me a new ladder in a new situation and I will probably find some excuse and go and make the coffee, but, strangely, the regular horrors cease to horrify. The daily ladder is just part of what I do and I can climb thirty feet up onto the deck, when the boat is on land, and look down quite calmly. The vertigo simply doesn't happen.

Sailing-Yacht *Trompeta*, Spanish for trumpet, is a forty-two foot Hallberg Rassy fibre-glass sloop. One mast, triangular sails, roller-reefing jib and standard, haul it up the hard way, drop it down all over the deck in a mess if it's stormy, mainsail. Modern, quite expensive as these things go, smart and comfortable. She is a cruising yacht, not a racer. Broad-beamed, roomy, robust. Cannot capsize. Might turn over, but would come up again, John says. She sleeps six, or seven at a pinch, eight if you like playing sardines. She is John's dream-come-true.

John wants to sail round the world. He sold his house, bought *Trompeta* in Sweden after his retirement and his divorce and brought her to Britain.

I was still firmly at work, nearing retirement but with no thought of leaving yet, even temporarily. I had no desire to circumnavigate, or even sail.

John and I did not expect to stay as an item and were more or less preparing to say, 'Nice knowing you', although we hoped that I might be able to visit him occasionally as he made his way around the globe.

I joined him and a friend, Mary, for a week in Spain. Mary is an experienced sailor and I was not expecting to do anything, just be a bit of elderly deck fluff. The night I arrived, *Trompeta* was moored bow-to. It was after midnight and the bow was very high above the jetty.

'You climb up like this,' said John, and demonstrated by putting first one foot above his head onto the deck, then the other, so that he hung below the bow like a monkey, and then swung himself up into the tangle of ropes and anchors around the foresail.

'Can I go home now?' I said.

He fetched a box and helped me up. Once up, I could not escape.

Over the next few days I learned some of the rudiments of sailing. At the close of the first day's sail, John patiently showed me how to tie clove hitches over the guard rail and put out the fenders along one side of the boat in exactly the right place to avoid damage as we came alongside the wharf. On the second day, as we came towards the dock in the next port of call, I thought, aha, I know how to do this, and I put out all the fenders, just so, without asking for guidance. I was very proud of my one-handed clove hitches. Too bad we approached from the other side.

The first time I took the helm it was of necessity. It was not one of my personal challenges. At the start of the third day we were sailing along nicely - bloody cold in my newly purchased inadequate wet weather gear but it was sunny and there were dolphins. Magic. They raced each other across the bows, back and forth, missing by inches and laughing as they came up for air.

And then John made the apparently sensible decision to go inside some island or other, between the island and the mainland, instead of the long way round the outside. He pointed out casually that we were now sailing on a *lee shore*. He and I were both keen for me to learn a bit of jargon. Being on a lee shore meant that if the wind came up, we would risk being swept sideways onto the rocks. Sure enough the wind came up. A violent storm. Quite exciting really. I felt safe with John. But he decided we were going too fast and needed to reef the mainsail.

He and Mary buckled up their safety harnesses and went out on the slippery heaving deck to take the mainsail down a bit and make it smaller. My job was to keep the boat heading into the wind to stop it moving forward, allow the sail to flap loosely, and to keep the boat off the rocks.

As a teenager I had sailed dinghies. I knew about pushing the tiller the wrong way and how to watch the little flag, the burgee, on top of the mast, to see how to line up the sails to go as fast as possible without capsizing. John's yacht has a wheel instead of a tiller and no burgee. It is somewhat bigger than a dinghy. The sails are enormous.

I fell into my place behind the wheel and waited for instructions. Heavy rain and spray were whipping my hair into my stinging eyes so I could not see John, and whisking away his voice so I could not hear him.

I grabbed the wheel as the boat lurched. I forgot everything I had once known about keeping head to wind. What should the sails look like? Which way should I steer if I want to go that way? Is it like a car or backwards like the tiller? How quickly should I compensate if the boat swings too far?

Not knowing made no difference. I was not hanging onto the wheel to steer the boat, no chance of that. I was hanging on to prevent being washed overboard. Rocks? Can't see them. Perhaps they'll go away.

'Well done,' John said, as he pried my rigor'd fingers from the wheel, 'isn't this grand?'

I went back to work, leaving John to sail to the Canary Islands and then across the Atlantic. Various friends joined him along the way.

Now, here we are in Venezuela, a brief holiday for me and a change of crew for John as he meanders around the Caribbean, exploring, while he waits for the best season to pop through the Panama Canal and out into the Pacific Ocean.

And, today, I am going to climb the mast. I would like *not* to be a wimp. Climbing the mast is a significant step in the de-wimping process. Surely if I can climb a mast I will be able to do anything. There cannot be worse horrors. Confront your worst fears and nothing can frighten you ever again.

Conditions are perfect. The weather forecast is good. The sea is glassy smooth. The yacht is tied securely to the wharf in a sheltered harbour, it is rocking only gently and the mast is hardly swinging.

John has fitted my granny step at the base of the mast. I couldn't even attempt to climb before. Without the extra step, I couldn't get my feet onto the first mast steps at shoulder height. John can reach up and grasp the second pair of steps, bring his knees up to his chest and put both feet on the first steps, pause in his familiar monkey-like way, and then pull himself up to standing. Good for him.

I have everything prepared: the right stretchy tee-shirt and shorts and gloves that won't stick or slip when wet with my sweat; the bosun's chair to prevent me falling when I slip; and my camera. I doubt if I will be able to let go with both hands and that is not part of the challenge but I'll take the camera just in case - maybe I can operate it with one hand, or my teeth.

OK I'm ready. Time to tell John. He's not busy. He's finishing his coffee. It is the best time of the day. I am wide awake, feel good, not too much caffeine. Calm, steady. Right. OK.

'John,' I call.

He looks up.

'I have decided . . .'

There is a thump on the hull and a rapid knocking. We both go to look. Three young men in smart heavy uniforms, in huge boots, carrying guns, are lined up along the quay. I don't understand the Spanish but it seems they want to search the boat. Routine, John assures me. Guns? Stowaways?

They remove their boots. That's nice of them.

PARALLEL MAGNOLIAS

'Hi Roxy, I've got your latest but it's gone wrong again. Can you send another one? Save it on a different memory stick first, not the hard drive perhaps, so it can't get muddled.'

Pete typed rapidly, sent the email and waited. He hoped she was on-line. She was.

'Hey Pete, what's a memory stick? No it's OK, I can guess. I'll get the vis and capture a new one and put all the autochromes in a different bank. I'm going out now, talk to you later.'

Roxanne and Pete had met on the Internet six months ago. That was a long time for both of them. Others had come and gone. Both were casually dating in 'real life'. They were both seventeen and planning to go to college, but this was getting serious, they could tell. They had so much in common. They laughed at the same jokes. They both liked Italy. Both wanted to study Renaissance History. Both had parents who were musicians. They liked the same classical music, art and theatre. Even jazz, although they did not have the same favourites. To his surprise, Pete did not know the names of the jazz players that Roxy gave, but he was only just beginning his collection. There must be more out there than he realised. Mind you, if there was one thing Pete had learned from Internet contacts, you couldn't safely make too many assumptions about what you really had in common until you met.

They had deliberately not told each other where they lived. They had decided to see if they could guess from the photos. He hoped she was not on the other side of the world. They were on the same time, and speaking English, if not the same slang. Somewhere in Africa, perhaps. He hoped not. He tried to keep his feelings under control, but didn't succeed. He wanted to be with her now.

They had had difficulty with sending attachments right from the start. Their word processors weren't compatible, messaging didn't work, attempts to send music were complete failures and now the photos weren't working properly. Roxanne couldn't download his photos. He was secretly glad of that, as he did not photograph well. The ones Roxy sent of herself were fine – a bit hazy perhaps, but enough for Pete to know he was certain to like her. It was the ones of her house that were giving trouble. When she tried to send a picture of her house, all he got was his photo of his own house back again.

Pete started to close down his computer, then decided to have another look at Roxanne's photos. She looked great. Bubbly. Cuddly. Good in . . ., hmm, better not go there. He looked for clues in the backgrounds of the pictures, but there were no cars and the scenes were too vague to make out landmarks. The interiors were all her bedroom. The gloriously untidy room could be anywhere. The huge paintings must be Monet. How had she managed to find such big posters? Her sound system and computer looked strange, but new models were coming out all the time and he hadn't looked in the shops lately. He used modern technology, but he was no computer nerd and he did not follow the crowd. He was curious about her odd way of talking sometimes. It wasn't a dialect or slang that he recognised, although he could work out the meanings easily enough. Perhaps her school had its own slang. She didn't know the computer jargon he used. That was the oddest thing. She was not ignorant of computers. Knew more about how they worked than he did. Surely, everyone knows what a memory stick is?

He brought up the photo of his house. How *had* that got in there with her pictures? Hey! That was weird. Looking carefully, he could see someone at an upstairs window. Had his mother been in the day he took the photo? He thought she'd been out at a rehearsal. He printed all the pictures and went downstairs. His mother was playing keyboard with headphones. He tapped her on the shoulder.

'Hi Mum. Look at these.'

'More pictures of Roxanne?'

He didn't need to keep this relationship secret any more.

'Yep. And one of you that you don't know about.'

His mother took the pictures and went through them.

'She's nice isn't she? Has that down-to-earth girl-next-door sort of look, but interesting at the same time. I've never seen hair done that way before. And her dress is most unusual.'

'Trust you to notice things like that.'

'Well, I won't ask you what you notice! When did you take this?'

She held up the picture of their house.

'Last week. I can see you in the window. Look.'

'Last week? You can't have. The magnolia hasn't come into flower yet.'

She pointed outside at the front garden.

'It's just about to bloom, be out in a day or two.'

They looked at the photo again. The magnolia was in full flower. Pete's mother fetched a magnifying glass and peered at the upstairs window.

'That's probably Roxanne – you can see the outline of her hair.'

'But that's my photo. It's our house.'

'It looks very much like it. And there aren't any others in this style. My great, great grandfather was an architect. He designed it for his first wife. When she died in 1895, he moved away. Our family came back here when my grandmother learned the story. I suppose he, or someone else, could have built a copy. I wonder where it is. Now, I want to know where she lives!'

They both rushed upstairs.

Disappointingly, there was no new message. Pete typed,

'Roxy, send more photos now and your address. No time for guessing now. Tell you why later.'

Pete did not sleep much that night. Strange dreams briefly interrupted his thoughts. The photo was his house. He was sure of it. Even allowing for the poor resolution of the pictures, he could see that the porch had the same misshapen paving stones.

When Roxanne's message came, she did not give her address. She had finally found how to open the attachment with Pete's photos. Pete hardly noticed the things she said about how great he looked. He saw only, ' . . . but when your chromes finally came up on the canvas, the one of the house was just the one I sent of our house here. I can't think what's going wrong.'

He typed back, 'Look at the magnolias', then sat back and waited.

Her reply came back immediately.

'Hey, weird. On the canvas, the magnolias are not in bloom, but I know they were in full flower when I captured them. I'm sending more now and my address. Stand by.'

The first photo formed line by line on the screen. Pete and his mother watched as the roof of the house, their house surely, came into view, then the magnolias, the first flowers already fading, and Roxanne sitting on the porch, her hand resting on one of the oddly cut flagstones.

He sent, 'Got it. Stand by while I get my digital.'

He grabbed his camera and his mother's arm and they went out to the front. She took a photo of him on the porch, making sure the magnolia buds were clearly visible. Pete loaded the picture into the computer and sent it, with his address. Roxanne wasted no time.

'Hey, wierder. And look, our addresses are the same too, except for the carriage code. Must be two towns with the same name.'

But there weren't. When they fetched their atlases, the latitude and longitude matched. Same house, same place, same time. Only the magnolias were different. And their universes.

They were not related. It would have been too weird if they had turned out to be cousins, or children of the same parents or something. As far as they could tell, their universes had split apart at the time that Pete's great, great grandmother died in 1895. Roxanne was able to trace the story of the architect who moved away. Her family had bought the house then and stayed ever since. Up to that point, their histories were the same.

After that, as Pete and Roxanne now discovered, nothing was the same. For Roxanne there had been no World wars, no Hitler, no USSR. Russia was ruled by Anatolia, grand-daughter of Emperor Nicholas II.

Strange, they reflected, what you do not think to discuss by email when you are dating.

They were the same age. They liked Shakespeare, Beethoven, Turner and Chung Mee green tea. They shared the same sense of humour. They lived in the same house. They could never meet.

When the shock subsided, they consoled each other if their parallel universes could use the same Internet, maybe they would find a way.

WHY I DON'T GO JOGGING ANY MORE

There was an old jogger called Hatherly
Who went out each morning and Saturday
She ran up and down
And all round the town
With her bosoms going flapperty, flapperty.

J.E.E.

I fiddled with my earring. My ear was getting sore. A man paused, looking, and I fiddled again but he walked on. A tap on my shoulder made me jump.

'Hello, Susan? His hair was strawberry blond and curly. He'd said short, fair. He gave me a peck on each cheek. Wow no holding back here. His face smelt faintly spicy. Promising.

'Hello.' I said.

His briefcase was charcoal grey, not black, and the unusual initials J.E.E. were embossed in the leather, not gold. The raincoat was not folded and it was navy, not beige. Men are hopeless with colours.

I was wearing the dark red suit with calf length skirt that suited me so well, with black sling-backs to show off my ankles. The butterfly earrings were silver, orange and dark red, striking against my black hair. Hard to miss.

'That ear looks sore, Susan. Just a minute I may have something that would help.'

He rummaged in his briefcase, found a tube, squeezed out a blob of cream, reached over, took out my earring, massaged cream into my earlobe, and replaced the earring. I did not object. He had a gentle touch and his hand smelt fresh and sweet. I wanted to move my cheek to brush against his palm.

'Where shall we go?' I said.

'Your choice,' he said.

I hesitated. Waterloo Station was a favourite meeting spot, plenty of scope for first dates, difficult to choose.

'We could go to the bar in the Festival Hall,' he suggested.

I breathed deeply. It was precious to me as it was somewhere Rob and I used to go, but this man already seemed different from the usual date.

I wasn't looking for a long-term partner, no-one could replace Rob, but I needed some kind of social life. Dating via the *Eye Love* ads in *Private Eye* was fun. I always told my sister where I was going. Carried my mobile phone. If she didn't hear from me by 11.30, she would phone.

J.E.E. was offering me a drink.

'What do you do these days?' he asked.

I had told him on the phone. And what did he mean by *these days*? Men! He had told me he was a solicitor so I asked about his hobbies. He was looking at me strangely. Embarrassed, I changed the subject; there was an exhibition in the foyer so I asked him if he knew the photographer.

'No,' he said, 'but interesting as it would be to chat, I'd like to get down to business.'

I froze. What could he mean? Our business *was* chatting: making conversation while we sized each other up; deciding whether there was any point in meeting again. Few survived the first five minutes.

'I need your help,' he said, 'with Anne's things.'

Anne? He was wearing a wedding ring. He had told me he was single, never married, why would he lie about that? There was no point giving such obvious false information, it made meeting a waste of time.

'My help, Jeremy? How can I help you?'

'James,' he corrected, puzzled.

'Sorry. I have a bad memory for names.'

I fished out my diary: Jeremy Edward Evans.

'Your name is James?'

'Yes. I know we haven't seen each other for ten years but what …'

He tailed off into confused silence.

'Solicitor?'

'Doctor, and you're not Susan?'

'Yes, I'm Susan, but who . . . ?'

'Anne's sister. You look different but time, you know . . . I gave her earrings like those.'

We stared at each other. He was the first to stand.

'We'd better hurry.'

We ran to the station and began to search. His phone battery was flat. I handed him my mobile. He dialled, listened, dialled again, left a text message. We stood.

'Can we sit somewhere?' Running in these shoes was not good.

We walked to a bench.

'My wife died. Cancer.'

'I'm sorry.'

My mobile rang and after a brief conversation, James gave me back my phone.

'Must go. Nice meeting you, Susan. Sorry to have wasted your evening. Hope you catch up with Jeremy.'

'Lovely to meet you too, James.'

We shook hands. I might catch the next train if I was lucky.

'Excuse me. Your name isn't Susan is it?' A man barred my way.

Beige raincoat folded neatly over his arm; black briefcase; gold initials, J.E.E.; straight short fair hair.

'Er, no. Sorry.'

I ran down the escalator and caught my train with a minute to spare.

For the first time, I had wanted to kiss someone other than Rob. I should wait a day or two, then phone. I would phone him tomorrow. Now. No. I didn't get his phone number. Or his last name.

Perhaps he would phone me. No, he couldn't. Wait a moment, would his calls to his Susan still be in her mobile's memory? Ah ha! Her number will be in my mobile. No, it isn't. Spit! Stupid phone! I knew I should have replaced it.

I would not sleep tonight. How many days would it take before I stopped running to the phone every time it rang? Why would he ring, even if he could? He probably didn't even notice me, once he realised I was not his sister-in-law.

I might phone Jeremy after all. Something to do. He didn't look too bad. Yes he did. He was still there. Must be desperate. My mobile rang. I jumped. It was my sister.

'I know it's not 11.30, but I want to go to bed early. Can you talk? Any good?'

'Wrong man.'

'Aren't they all?'

'Tell you tomorrow. Thanks for checking that I'm safe. Sleep well. Goodnight, Sis.'

'G'night.'

I turned off the phone. Don't even hope. Forget it.

Eventually we reached my station and I walked slowly to my car. Driving at night, I always turn on my mobile. It bleeped. There was a txt.

'If Jmy not 2 taste c u again? J.E.E.'

TRIPOS

Familiar interstellar icons label the various vending machines in the deserted docking station. Some leaf patterns are strange but all have standard nutrition advice. I touch a few illustrations and take a tray of assorted items.

Climbing is my passion, which is why I have been picked to prepare the guidebook for this unexplored, un-named mountainous planet. It has a number that identifies its place in the galaxy. That is all. My editor let slip that their previous travel writer did not land, or stay long enough to find out anything more than it now boasts a docking station. The origins of this are unknown. My entry was automated.

Apparently, the spectacular rocky outcrops cover almost two-thirds of the planet with little variation from equator to poles and there are no intelligent life forms. It is like the wildest areas of the Badlands of South Dakota. Very little prairie. The remaining third is water. Close by, the rocks are sharp and steep, good for climbing if you have the gear. Further away there are softer, twisted forms where wind and sand have whittled intricate outlines. In places, fluctuating iridescent bubbles emerge from crevices.

I sense something behind me. I whirl round.

The furry head keeps swivelling like an owl's, revealing three eyes but no visible nose, mouth or ears. It stands as tall as me. I register that it is completely covered in tortoiseshell fur. No clothing. Natural, like a cat.

It doesn't look dangerous but my heart races. It is beautiful. It has three arms, almost equally spaced and three legs. The creature pauses, a perfectly balanced tripod, and holds out one of its arms in a slow measured movement as if in greeting. Small folds appear around the two eyes that are facing me and I can hear a kind of purring. I think maybe it is smiling, or even laughing. I take the proffered hand and the purring deepens.

'Welcome to our planet Tripos,' it says softly, and I see its eye folds ripple.

I stare into two of the eyes. I am lost in them. A stunningly beautiful intelligent cat.

Abruptly the head swivels so that a different pair of eyes faces me. The spacing is different and it is hard to look into both. The mesmerising mood is broken.

'Welcome,' it says again. 'My name is Xhanthar.'

'I'm Sam,' I say.

'You are not like previous visitors, Sam,' Xhanthar says, 'you have not come with machines and weapons. Such smooth skin. Will you take off your fabrics and let me see you?'

I laugh out loud and it retreats a little.

'Sorry,' I say. 'I didn't mean to startle you. In my culture it is not customary to undress within a few minutes of meeting.'

'But the visuals? Many of them are without fabrics.'

'Ah yes. No doubt you have pictures of naked humans. But we usually like to get to know each other a bit better before…'

I am a frequent traveller. On Earth, and other planets where humans are common, I am constantly on the lookout for possible sexual encounters. I'm unattached, free to explore. But I have never yet found myself attracted to a non human being, though there have been ample opportunities. What is going on here? A three-armed, three-legged, three-eyed cat? But it is not a cat. No tail. It is as tall as me. It speaks. It is lovely in the extreme. I want to stroke it. My feelings are not sexual, well not exactly, but I want to feel its fur against my skin. I don't even know if it is male or female.

'Please, let me finish my breakfast,' I say, 'and then perhaps you can take me exploring.'

'Yes, of course. There is no hurry.'

Xhanthar names each of the foods, and tells where they have come from and how they are cultivated. The textures and flavours are pleasant, not unlike those I have tried elsewhere, which is not surprising as nearly all the vegetable matter is grown from imported seeds, in hydroponic farms under the rainbow bubbles, although there are some indigenous fungi, mosses, lichens and grasses, enough to have supported the evolution of animals.

I don't know why but I get the feeling that there is something Xhanthar is not telling me. And why did my predecessor leave so abruptly? What was it that had been visible from the spacecraft? Why was there fresh food in the vending machines if they don't welcome visitors? Who built the docking station?

Xhanthar tells me to bring some of my lighter climbing equipment and then we are ready to venture outside and explore.

As we climb, Xhanthar quizzes me thoroughly and gives me a potted account of land formations and evolution. Not all that different in principle from Earth except for the endless rocks and the survival only of tripartite creatures that are well suited to climbing. Xhanthar glides swiftly and easily over rocks that present me with difficult challenges. Useful for parties, too, I think.

'What's your family like?' I ask eventually. 'Parents? Brothers? Sisters? Partner?'

'Three parents,' Xhanthar replies. 'The usual. Two siblings. The third will come soon.'

'Boys or girls?' I ask.

Xhanthar purrs. 'We do not understand your concept of male and female. You have only two kinds and you have strong expectations about how each kind should dress or walk or take its place in society. That must be hard on those who do not wish to fit in with conventions.'

'How many kinds do you have, then? Three? Like everything else?'

'Oh no,' Xhanthar replies, with no trace of irony, 'eighteen.'

'Eighteen!' I must have shouted in my surprise as Xhanthar swivelled away, eyes shut briefly, before regaining composure.

'Eighteen is good,' Xhanthar said. 'Too many for expectations. The boundaries are blurred.'

'But when you have children?' I want to ask about having sex but I can't get my head round that.

'Most of us can be either mother or father as we choose. We can be mother for one child, father to another, perhaps. The nearest on Earth is hermaphrodite, I believe, but we have many different permutations and combinations.'

'Everyone can be mother and father?'

'No, that is not possible. Some are mothers only, or fathers only. Some are what you would call only neuter. But if they are the third parent, that no longer has importance. All can suckle the young.'

'Oh,' I say lamely. Simpler with only two, I think, although I know there are variations even on Earth. 'And what are you, Xhanthar?'

'Can't tell you.' The purr comes out in hiccups. Definitely laughing. 'Like taking your fabrics off, we don't reveal that until …'

'But how do you know who . . .'

'Doesn't matter, does it? Unless you want to parent.'

I could understand that. It didn't matter to me either except that I always knew in advance. Well, almost always.

By now we have traversed the region of hard rock I had seen from the dock and reached the softer eroded formations. Here I begin to see evidence of life: scratches on the rocks around the cracks and crevices, levelled areas like back yards, a few plants.

'This is where we live,' Xhanthar confirms. 'I'll take you to my Burrow to meet my family.' Again, there is that guarded tone in the soft voice. What was there to hide? Is my guide a mere kitten, with huge flesh-eating 'big cat' parents who eat animals without telling their children and prey on unsuspecting travellers?

Driven by curiosity and, if I'm honest, desire, I follow as Xhanthar ducks into a partly concealed entrance that opens into a light airy cave, sunlight directed down through roughly carved sun tunnels. Several furry tripod people are grouped, apparently expecting me.

They introduce themselves. They are different colours. One parent is, perhaps, a little bigger than Xhanthar but not by much. There are kittens - I cannot call them anything but that. They tumble over each other, play hide and seek around the legs of their elders. Pounce on anything that moves. Was I to be dinner tonight?

After the opening pleasantries I ask where they cook. Perhaps that would give me a clue.

'Oh, we don't cook,' the black one answers. 'We eat all our food raw. We don't have the technology for cooking. Or fuel. Our engineering is in its infancy but we are beginning to mine now and learn how to manufacture and build. Soon we . . .'

'Raw?'

'That's partly why we eat only plants,' Xhanthar says.

'We've not evolved for meat anyway,' a tabby cuts in, as if reading my thoughts. 'You, for instance, would be completely indigestible.'

They all burst out in hiccupping purring, great creases appearing around their eyes.

'We can see you are concerned,' the tabby says suddenly. 'You are right. We shouldn't tease you.'

'I'll explain now,' Xhanthar says. 'Your planet is planning to invade, now that it is known that we have rich mineral deposits. Will you help us stop them, Sam.'

'Me? I wouldn't know how. I'm a writer, not a spy or assassin.'

'But you can write. Tell your people the truth about us.'

'I. . . I'd rather stay here. With . . . with you,' I falter.

'We know. We understand,' the tabby says, 'and we'd love you to stay. But first we need you to go home and fight for us. We'll help you.'

'But even if I could somehow prevent an invasion for a while, there would be others, surely?' I say.

'You will give us the time we need to build our defences.'

'And this will become like every other planet in the known world,' I grieve, 'instead of this unspoilt, beautiful and wild place.'

'We cannot prevent change, but we can try to slow it down a little.'

Unbuttoning my shirt, Xhanthar rubs soft fur against my bare skin. The sensation and natural scent are overpowering and for a moment we are both lost in the embrace.

EVE BITES FIRST

This is Paradise. Everything in Paradise is perfect.

Adam strolls slowly across the meadow. Eve, on his shoulders, eggs him on.

'Faster!'

He ambles, not quite so slowly.

'Faster! Faster!

He jogs. Unhurriedly. They reach the river. They swim. They eat. Adam collects some perfect stones from the perfect stream to add to his perfect collection then falls asleep.

Adam is gorgeous. Perfect, naturally.

Is he tall? Maybe. He has no system of measurement. Let's say he's your ideal height. Blue eyes? Why not? Let's give him plenty of recessive genes. So he is blond, with just a hint of red. Straight or curly? You choose. Long hair? He hasn't thought of cutting it. Beard? Naturally, as he hasn't worked out how to shave. If this is not quite to your taste, then you'll have to adjust your ideal to suit the technology of the time. He also has lots of chest hair and quite a bit on his shoulders, and his belly. Not to mention further down. His belly hair is soft and strokeable.

Adam is strong. Broad chest and back, lots of muscles, not tending to fat. Neat bum. He doesn't have to *work out* to maintain that body - this is Paradise. He eats slowly, methodically, one thing at a time. He is vegetarian (because the rabbits keep out of his way). He digests fast, having a perfect metabolic rate, and farts, naturally. He's a big blond bear: warm, comfortable to cuddle, protective. He's never angry, never upset, never sad, never disgusted. Never excited. Adam is a bear-skin rug. He takes up a lot of room. He gets under Eve's feet.

Eve is perfect too. Adam doesn't notice; naturally. Eve is everything Adam is not. She plays with the rabbits. Then she eats them.

We'll give her dominant genes. Brown hair, brown skin, brown eyes. Adaptation to a hot climate. Slow, efficient metabolic rate. Body reserves for stamina. Curves. She is sleek and glossy as an otter. A panther. Hidden strength. Air of laziness. Watchful, ready to spring and glide. Vital, curious, inventive, adventurous. (Or so she would have you believe.)

'Adam!' Eve's voice rings out over the clearing.

'Yes, dear?'

'I've made a drink, if you want some.'

'Thanks. Great.'

Adam sorts his stones in straight lines. He can't count yet, of course, but each line resembles the next, or makes a geometrical pattern. They are arranged according to size. One row is the size of hens' eggs. Some *are* hens' eggs. Adam has not realised the full potential of eggs - if one of them cracks open and spills its fluid contents at his feet, he replaces it. Eve likes hers fried, sunny-side-up.

Adam has not considered cooking his food. Eve has but she resists the temptation. She cooks only for herself; except the occasional drink - it's nice to share sometimes. However, she does not waste her painstakingly peeled, roasted and ground coffee beans on Adam. She finds a substitute for him: a simpler brew, of barley and hops, which, unheeded, will be cold, fermented even, by the time he remembers to turn up. Time, you will appreciate, has no meaning for Adam.

'Adam?'

'Yes, dear?'

'What's that for?'

'What?'

'That.' (Their vocabulary is somewhat limited, as you can imagine.)

'Oh that. You know what that's for. You've seen me.'

'I know that. But I can do that. What else is it for?'

'I don't know, dear.' And Adam goes back to re-arranging his rocks.

Eve sighs, 'What have I done to deserve this?'

She climbs up into her favourite tree. She munches a slice of apple. She knows God is watching. God knows she knows.

Along comes the serpent.

'Why don't you give sssssome of that to Adam?' the serpent beguiles.

'Sssss off. It's mine.'

A rabbit rolls exhausted from the back of its playmate and flops over on its side. Eve strokes her breasts. She hasn't had them long. They appeared one day. They feel nice. She has tried to get Adam to touch them but he just grunts and plays with his pebbles. Perhaps she will offer him just a tiny bite of apple.

BABY SHOES

'Baby shoes for sale, never worn.' Gerry typed out the brief advertisement, added the price and contact information, printed several copies and prepared to take them to suitable places: two local supermarkets, the village post office, the nearest library, charity shops. She made extra copies in case she thought of somewhere else on the way round.

It would pull at people's heartstrings, she reflected. Everyone would assume the baby had died. Such a sad thing the death of a baby. Things like that - it was hard to imagine how horrible it felt until it happened to you. You thought you knew how it would feel and would even say to the person concerned 'I know how you feel.' But you didn't. You couldn't. It really was better not to say anything much in those circumstances, just make comforting noises and offer practical help if it seemed appropriate.

Would knowing the baby had died make people more likely to buy the shoes, she wondered. Or would they be superstitious and not want to own such tainted objects in case it brought them bad luck. She needed the money. It wouldn't be much but every little helped these days. She could buy more useful items.

Gerry didn't approve of baby shoes as they could damage delicate little feet particularly if the baby was encouraged to stand and walk before it was ready. She liked those all in one babygrows with feet that keep the baby warm without the need for socks or shoes. She sniffed back a tear. Thinking of dead babies made her very sad. She didn't really want to make other people sad too. That wasn't fair.

She tore up the ads and re-typed: For sale, unused baby shoes. Unwanted present.

THINGS TO DO EVERY DAY

Every day I shall paint a picture
Composition, contrast, colour, impact
Head, hand, heart

Every day I shall read a poem
For love of sounds
Hidden meanings, lasting thoughts

Every day I shall dance
Pounding my feet, whirling, leaping
Stretching my muscles
Lifting my soul

Every day I shall sing a song
Practise scales and arpeggios
For sheer joy
Knowing I will annoy my neighbours
And my cats will try to comfort me

Every day I shall walk in the garden
Talk to flowers
Plant something new
Move weeds to better places
Train over enthusiastic climbers
Where they suffocate slow shy shoots

Every day I will write
A story, poem, play
With words, people, places, plots,
Secrets.
They wait inside my head
Like an angel in stone
For this sculptor to find them.

NO MILK TODAY

Frowning, Gilbert put his phone back in his waistcoat pocket and prodded the cow's udder again. The cow looked at him balefully. He ought to know what was wrong but forty years as a neurosurgeon had not prepared him for this. As he heard car tyres on the gravel he got up stiffly and turned, gritting his teeth. His frown turned to horror.

'You, Dominic! I wasn't expecting *you*. Where's Charles?'

'Hello, brother. Not expecting me, eh? Thought I was still safely in New Zealand? I'm Charles's new partner. Hoped you'd call soon. Nice little retirement project you've got, eh? How's Daisy here? What do *you* think is wrong?'

Gilbert's eyes narrowed at the obvious taunt. He hated having to call in the vet at the best of times and to get his younger brother was too much.

'Dominic, be my guest, you go first,' he said, trying to regain some dignity.

'OK, bro. But tell me, what symptoms?'

'No milk. Out of sorts.'

'For how long?' Dominic was smiling.

'How long? How should I know? The milkmaid told me this morning, said I should get the cow examined.'

'Milkmaid?' Dominic chortled. He patted the cow on the rump. 'Show me round your lovely 18th Century organic farm,' he said, 'I want to know how you do it.'

'You do?' Gilbert brightened. 'Come with me then.' He sent a text and frowned at the phone for a moment. 'Deirdre will join us in a minute.'

'What you got?' Dominic asked, 'cows, sheep, arable?'

'Bit of everything we can manage,' Gilbert replied proudly, 'good mix of animals, chickens, ducks, rotation of crops, manure for fertilizer, wind generator, composting toilet. Self sufficient and sell the surplus.'

'Don't need to make a profit, then?' his brother teased, resisting the temptation to make some jibe about the toilet and selling the surplus.

'No, we don't, not really,' Gilbert answered seriously. 'Just so long as we can feed ourselves, pay the manager and the others and not make a loss. Deirdre's really good at the accounts. Well she should be. She didn't want to retire until we actually found this farm, then fell in love with it. Her project really. Reckoned we could make a go of it with her accountancy and my medical expertise.'

'Medical expertise?' Dominic smiled broadly.' Well you should be good at the mad cow disease – good neurological stuff that.'

'Yes, of course,' Gilbert stiffened. 'Haven't had any of that, fortunately.'

'Show me the cows. Any others off colour?'

'You don't think it could be mad cow do you?' Gilbert frowned more deeply than ever.

'You enjoying your retirement?' Dominic asked, suddenly concerned.

Gilbert looked up at him, as disconcerted as always by the difference in their heights, doubly disconcerted by the unexpected kindness in his brother's voice.

'Since you ask, no,' he replied. 'What *is* wrong with my cow?'

'Nothing,' Dominic replied, 'she's pregnant. Good to see you Gilbert.'

'Ah . . . yes . . . good . . . you too, Dominic.'

I LEFT MY WOMB IN CHAGUARAMUS

'How soon can you get here?' The voice is friendly, concerned.

Using the pay phone at the boatyard gate, I have asked for a moderately urgent appointment with a gynaecologist and have my diary handy.

Startled, I stammer that the earliest would be whenever the next bus into Port of Spain can get me there. The buses are frequent, if unpredictable. Just need to find John, somewhere among the hundreds of yachts in the marina, tell him I'm going, and grab some flip flops.

'That's OK', the voice reassures me, 'we'll be expecting you.'

If I lie flat on my back, the swelling from my fibroid looks and feels like a hard boiled egg. It doesn't hurt but I am bleeding copiously again, felt sick and tired all yesterday and am panicking that serious consequences could occur when sailing miles from anywhere.

Heavily padded, I enjoy as usual the minibus drive along the coast and into town. It is not yet too hot to walk comfortably and I find the surgery without trouble.

Unpadded, I leak blood all over the upright examination couch which tilts back like a dentist's chair, only more so.

'You shouldn't be bleeding like this . . . I'm afraid there's no alternative . . . Too late for hormone treatment . . . Oh dear . . . Take these pills . . . Take this letter to the hospital.'

My feet indicate I am severely anaemic. I can't imagine how the doctor can tell through the ingrained dirt but she apologises that she can't operate this Saturday, we'll have to wait a week until the iron pills have done their stuff.

Across the road I have a blood test that confirms the anaemia, make an appointment with the anaesthetist for the next day, and for ultrascan the day after. The decision has been taken out of my hands. I have tried to let my body sort itself out but it can't. Fibroids shrink after menopause but that could be a long way off.

I favour having it done now, here in Trinidad. I could go back to the UK; but I think of my house, under the care of carefree son, and can't face the cobwebs. Or my sister insisting she will look after me. There's a 'flu epidemic in the UK. Hospital beds are scarce. Private care here in a small clinic will be about the same as the airfare.

Waiting for my ultrasound, I have drunk eight cups of water since breakfast as instructed, and the doctor is delayed. If I don't pee soon I shall burst. Hesitantly, since I don't want to interfere with the scan, I ask the receptionist if I may. 'Yes, fine,' she says, 'just go on drinking.'

Much later, the doctor arrives. He runs the scanner over my belly and turns the screen around so I can watch. My fibroid measures 11 cm by 9½ - somewhat bigger than an egg. My uterus is swollen to roughly the equivalent of eighteen weeks of pregnancy. I almost expect it to kick. Friends over the years have variously described their fibroids as the size of grapefruit or melons. The bigger the better. There is point scoring in the size of one's fibroids and cysts. I am up there with the best of them.

When I escape and pee, it takes ages. Pure joy. Such are the real pleasures in life.

Back at the yacht, I wail that I have no such thing as a nightdress and Carol buys me a white cotton one in the market. Phillis lends me a beautiful Chinese long satin shirt. Friends call to wish me luck. Rosie brings me raisin bread, freshly made in her bread-maker. Another yachtie stops to ask if anything is wrong – she did not know us but had seen John cuddle me out on deck early in the morning. The live-aboard yachting community is like an old fashioned village. We enquire about blood donor tickets; I need two, I'm told, but better get a third to be safe. I'm grateful to the donors and rather glad I had all the proper inoculations.

The gynaecologist has drawn me a familiar picture. Bikini-line cut, removal of uterus and ovaries, vaginal reconstruction. Nothing new. Piece of cake. Couldn't be simpler. I nod, dumbly, obediently.

Wait a minute! Vaginal reconstruction? What a horrible expression. Suddenly I am no longer a woman. Why not do the whole job? Remove both my breasts as well, why don't they? Leave me as an android without any sexual features. Might as well, for all the sexual interest I feel. It's been a long time since I felt stirrings. It won't matter if ripping out my insides leaves me not feeling sexy; I won't notice the difference. Mind you, having no breasts might make a nice change from my current 'fuller' figure; I'd be able to wear Laura Ashley dresses.

I have left a trail of destruction. But no more. Think of all the money I will save. No more tampons, no more pads. No more new car-seat covers. No more new mattresses. The memory of one particular hotel bed brings a blush to my face. Recent shopping in Margarita had been a problem; no sooner had I changed my pads and set off to rejoin the others than I felt the familiar oozing warmth and had to return hastily to the public toilet. I don't know if the attendant recognised me but she looked as if she did.

What freedom. No more PMS. No more cravings. No more post-menstrual creative burst. Oh hell!

I respect the gynaecologist, Dr Phelps. Trinidadian, trained in the US. She may not probe my deeper feelings but she's practical, well-informed and skilled, comes highly recommended and asks all the right questions about my symptoms. I imagine she sees me as a sensible woman, one who knows she no longer needs her reproductive organs, accepts there is no choice and will eventually be thankful. I expect she's right. I'm not very frightened, but I am sad. And angry. I'm cross about the ovaries; they're not doing any harm. 'We don't want you back again in a year or two,' the doctor stops my protests. I want to scream and wail. I feel cheated. My body has let me down. I am outraged at the slash and burn tactics, the too-easy solution of surgery. 'It's just a bag. Throw it away.'

Hysterectomy is one of the most common surgical procedures. Why is it needed so often? Imagine, in mid-life, if nearly all penises developed fibroids and bled uncontrollably from time to time. What if the only remedy was to lop them off? 'It's only a tube, throw it away.'

'I've been waiting for you,' the anaesthetist smiles at me and calls for a replacement trolley and helps me transfer to it from the wheelchair. We are late because the designated trolley collapsed when the enormous porter leant on it instead of turning the handle to lower the back.

I am trolleyed into theatre. Dr Peters, gorgeous, married, is not a good driver and I have to keep my elbows well clear of the walls. I am helped onto the operating table. It would have been so much simpler to have walked and climbed up. But they have their policy. I tell them that when I had a D&C in England, I had to walk to theatre, down many flights of stairs. Several voices from behind my head chorus, well, that was a D&C. They refrain from adding, well, that was England.

Dr Peters asks, 'Where is Dr Phelps? Why does she always keep me waiting?' Dr Phelps is watching from the door and I suspect this is a well-rehearsed routine, but it makes me smile anyway. Dr Peters rubs alcohol on my hand and inserts the cannula. He says, 'You'll soon start feeling woozy.'

'I already am,' I think I reply.

It's all over. I have woken from some very sexy dreams. Watch out John! The catheter was removed ages ago. We've finished the blood transfusion and the saline drip came out yesterday. I have moved on from clear fluids and 'softs' to regular spicy chicken, chick peas and rice, and from pethadine to paracetamol. The dressings have been removed.

I've had all three units of blood. At first I was amused by the bubbles that kept appearing in the tube and watched as the senior nurse clipped the tube and flipped with her finger nails to send the bubbles back into the top.

Then, when I was alone, the bubbles began to move down again. Crime novels. Air into vein. Silent, undetectable murder. Panic! I pressed the call button. And again. Student nurse in spotless white overalls arrived. 'Look! Look!' She looked. 'Please,' I pleaded, 'you must stop the bubbles.' Nonchalantly, experimentally, she flipped the tube with her finger nails and the bubbles advanced more rapidly towards my hand because she had neglected to clamp the tube. She went out. I died.

She returned with a green-clad nurse. I lived. Much later I learned the air has to be under considerable pressure to cause harm. OK.

The first time I tried to get up, a red hot poker rammed through my middle. Assistant Nurse Cheryl went to get help, but returned to say Nurse Ali was busy with a labourer. 'What? Sod the workman!' Cheryl held me and comforted me. When I heard the baby yell, I registered. I was in the Maternity Ward. The labourer had given birth. I heard someone sing out, 'What you had?' and the reply, 'a boy'.

Moments later Nurse Ali popped in and the welcome jab in my buttock soon brought relief. I reflected that I'd be useless under torture.

Now, I must walk the length of the corridor every few hours. The day old babies are delightful, so small, so relaxed in sleep, so individual already. A visitor asks which is my baby. I brush back my grey hair, think of my hulking sons and smile.

Because we're sailors, living on board, Dr Phelps insists on keeping me in a day or two longer than usual. On the day I'm discharged we arrange the taxi to coincide with the low tide so I won't have to climb so high to get back on board.

Friends welcome me back. Someone brings me her parrot to entertain me. The parrot walks up and down my arms, tries to snuggle inside my blouse, sits on my head. It hurts to laugh. I think I feel fine and look great so I'm a bit surprised by all the solicitousness. I'm not used to it. When the photos of me and the parrot are developed, they show a grey, wan invalid. We must wait at least six weeks before we sail.

Before the op I had a generous tum. I've been meaning to do something about this for ages, but you know how it is. Now, I have a tight scar line and my belly hangs over it in a droopy pleat. The scar may be hidden by a bikini, the belly would look ridiculous. Can't do anything about it, they all say. Dr Phelps says if you show me a woman over fifty with a flat stomach then I'll show you her tummy tuck. Hmm, well, we'll see.

For Christmas, John and I gave each other, to share, a digital camera and a Dremel miniature drill set. I adore the drill and all its fiddly little attachments. It drills, cuts, grinds, sands, scrapes, polishes . . . you name it, it does it. I'm not sure what I want to do with it, but it's fantastic.

Now, there's a thought. Perhaps I could find the right bits to give myself a tummy tuck.

AUTUMN WISHES

'Look there!' A wisp of thistledown drifted past. 'Can you see the fairies?'

Jessica caught the thistledown and examined it carefully. With a touch that was delicate for a five-year old, she untangled the seeds, lifted each one to her lips and blew. Each miniature parachute wafted on its way. The children looked at me curiously, solicitously, not quite pityingly.

'Yes Great Grandma.' Seven-year old Anthony pointed to a twinned sycamore key twirling in the breeze. 'And that's another I suppose.'

'I expect so,' I said, 'the fairies are everywhere. You just have to know how to look.'

I had overheard Marilyn, the youngest of my grandchildren, telling her son and daughter not to mind what Great Grandma said.

'She's very old. She sees things. Try to humour her. And make sure she doesn't walk too far. If anything happens, phone me.'

Her mobile was in my bag along with my sketchbook and pencils. I would not want to walk far. When the children stopped to play, I would sit and draw. Just as I used to.

As I walked, holding a child by each hand, memories came flooding back. I loved these Cornish moors. I loved September, my birthday month, when the breezes were just beginning to get sharp and the fruit was starting to swell and ripen. I knew all the wild berries, the leaves, flowers, fungi. And the fairies that belonged to each.

I showed Jessica and Anthony how to find the pale green satin hazelnuts with their curly calyx caps, hiding shyly under the leaves. It would be a few weeks yet before the nuts turned brown and were ripe enough to crack open and eat. We found woody nightshade with juicy, tempting, green and red berries. Not poisonous like the deadly nightshade, but not good for eating. There were large swollen rosehips and clusters of haws, signalling a harsh winter to come. We paused to listen to rustling under the hedge. A tiny shrew came cautiously out, then scampered back when Anthony sneezed.

It was a long time since I'd visited my home village. It was thoughtful of Marilyn and Paul to invite me to join them on this holiday, now that Ted has passed away.

When Ted and I were courting, we used to walk on the moors and rest on the dry soft moss. I would weave fairies out of strands of dry leaves and grass: he whittled twigs into mischievous elves and pixies. We would give these to the young children or leave them on the hills to be found later.

I pointed towards the old oak. It was still standing, unperturbed by its advancing years.

'I'll sit here for a bit. You two go and play. Find things. Come and show me, if you like.'

'OK, Great Grandma.'

They wandered off. I lowered myself carefully to the ground, took out my sketchbook and moved until I could see a fragment, a space framed by oak twigs and leaves, a little above my head. Lit from behind by the sun, it would be just right for the Autumn Oak Leaf Fairy in long papery brown dress with wavy edges, gossamer wings. It was too difficult for me to paint any more, now that my eyes were failing and my fingers were stiff with arthritis, but I could still draw well enough. Looser lines than in my younger days. Softer focus. Elusive, subtle, like the fairies.

From time to time, the children returned to show me their treasures. They had prickly burrs caught in their socks. They had found fuzzy goosegrass and written their names on their sweaters with the tiny round seeds.

The sun was warm in the shelter of the tree. The fairy was nearly done. It was difficult to get her wings right as she kept wriggling. I put the finishing touches to her feet.

'Thanks, that's better. I thought you'd never finish,' she reprimanded, as she jumped down from the sketchbook onto my foot. She tucked herself into a loop in the long laces of my ancient walking boots and sat, swinging a little, her skirt lifting in the breeze.

'Now,' she drawled, 'what d'ya want?'

'Want?'

'Yes, you know, three wishes and all that, but please be quick, the kids need me.'

'The children need you?'

'Yes, Jess and Tone. They think they don't believe in fairies, but secretly they'd like to. If they could catch a glimpse of me now, everything would be all right.

'Then that must be one of my wishes - that they catch a glimpse of you. I'd like that.'

'Oh, right. Good idea. What else?'

'Gracious. I've no idea. I don't want for anything. I've had a good life. I have my health. My children seem happy enough, in their own fashion. All my grandchildren are making their way, with families or careers, or both, perhaps they'd like . . .'

The fairy yawned.

'Awh, come on. Gimme a break. What do you want?' She slid off my shoe and onto the ground and stood, hands on hips. Demanding.

'I don't know. Wait! I'd like Ted to be here. I miss him.'

'Is that a wish?' The fairy looked upset.

'No! No, of course not. I mustn't wish for Ted to come back. It's not right to wish for things that cannot be, only for those that might, if you want them enough.'

'So?'

'I know - I'd like Ted to be able to see me and know that I'm happy.'

'He knows. You don't have to wish for that.'

'Oh. Thank you.'

'Don't thank me. I don't make the rules. Come on. Hurry up. We haven't got all day. What's so hard about making a wish? You didn't have this problem when you were a child.'

'You remember me? You're right. I had no problem at all making wishes. There were so many things to want. So many unknowns. So many possibilities.'

'And which of them came true?'

Which, indeed? What had I wished for? To have long hair down to my waist? That wish didn't last long. I cut it all off in a tantrum, one unforgettable morning. Can't have wanted that very badly. To be glamorous and rich and famous? No, I liked a quiet life. To marry and have children? To drive a tractor? Travel round the world? Go to the moon?

I closed my eyes. I heard the fairy open her wings.

'Don't go away yet, please. I'll tell you in a minute.'

What had I dreamed of as a child? What had I achieved with my life? I had wished to be an artist and become a moderately successful illustrator for children's books. I had wished for a prince and found one. Ted was a skilled carpenter, a restorer of antiques, and as gentle and loving with people as he was with the furniture. We had travelled extensively in our later years together, exploring the Old World and the New. He died peacefully in my arms. That was one wish I had no right to make, but I'm glad it came true. I had wished for three daughters, but didn't really mind, and had one daughter and two sons. Those were the big wishes.

What about the little wishes? What was left? What did I still want? There really was nothing left to wish for. I must be nearly at the end of my life; I would be ninety-six tomorrow. I had all I desired and, what's more, had learned to achieve what I wanted without the help of the fairies. I was pleased she remembered me. I may not need her help any more, but I had not forgotten her.

I heard a rustle beside me. Was the fairy waiting?

'Sshh! She's asleep. Put them down, here, like this. We need some more. We'll make a magic circle round her. She'd like that.'

'Look there's a fairy.'

'Don't be silly, it's just Great Grandma's drawing.'

'No, it's real, it moved its wings. Watch.'

I opened my eyes. Jessica was holding my sketchbook, swaying it gently from side to side.

'Look, she's moving, Great Grandma. She's trying to fly.'

'Let her go,' I said, 'hold the page up to the breeze so she can fly away.'

Jessica lifted the sketchbook up and flapped it. There was a brief shimmer of light.

'You must make a wish. I'm sure they'll still work if I give them to you. One each. Close your eyes. Don't tell anyone what you wish for and if you want it badly enough, you will make it come true, even if it seems far too difficult at the moment.'

When they opened their eyes again the fairy had gone. There was just a hazy sketch of a gap in the oak twigs, lit from behind by the September sun.

DUST

Dr Elizabeth Rictus sat stooped over her desk like a desiccated praying mantis, elongated legs entwined under the bespoke orthopaedic swivelling office chair, elegant long fingers stretched over the keyboard. Her long painted nails would have made typing difficult but they were needed only to hit a few strategic keys before activating the voice recognition software.

Dr Rictus tapped in her initials, selected today's favoured username from a list of anagrams and watched two more dots add themselves to the row representing her hidden password. She waited the briefest of moments as the website calculated her matches. She had one thousand matches available. Some, unknown to the website, were no longer viable. Her profile stated that she was an historian. Why would she lie? It wouldn't appeal to all men but she didn't want all men. She was taller than average, fit, active and *very* comfortable. She made sure that her photographs showed her luxurious home to its best advantage. There would be men who would wish to marry her for the house alone. She did not hide the fact that the building was in a remote part of the Fells where mobile phones did not work.

She selected a few likely matches as favourites. Waited to see who responded. Dusted the house while she waited. Needed to dust. While the builders had been busy, she had developed a most irritating allergy to dust.

Three responses. A good number. She chose one and tapped on 'send an email'. Relaxed, swivelled and dictated. She told him a good deal about herself: her failed marriage, disabled son, daughter in Australia, house rules for the singles parties she organised. She could let the words flow. At the end of two crammed pages she stopped to allow him to catch up. There would be a few voice recognition errors but if he was as intelligent as his profile suggested, he would be able to work out the intended meanings.

The more intelligent the better, she had found. Not streetwise. Or suspicious.

He responded in kind: his expensive divorce, his craving for adventure, his dream of moving to the countryside. He could touch type, he told her, with his eyes shut. An unusual and delicious image. She sent him more photos. He responded with details of his city flat.

Before long, he requested that they meet, had found it surreal to correspond so fully without really knowing each other. They arranged a date in a convenient pub half way between their respective homes. Better for you, he said, to be cautious. She did not contradict.

She allowed a suitable time to elapse after the appointed time, phoned in a message to the bartender that she was running late and would the single man wearing a dark blue overcoat with white carnation please either wait or make his way to her house.

She had good feelings about this one. She folded a duster on her desk, swivelled gently and waited.

GOSPEL ACCORDING TO AN UNKNOWN FRIEND

Jesus was a strange child. First, there were all those stories about him being born in a stable, but, you know, I went round all the inns in Bethlehem and not one of them remembered anything like that. They had tramps all the time, of course, but no-one remembered an old man and an innocent-looking girl, heavy with child, turning up and being taken to the stable. And all those shepherds and wise men? Media hype, I call it. But knowing what he was like later, it probably did happen that way.

He was special somehow. Quiet. Some of the rougher lads used to try and bully him, you know - hit him and ask him for food or money, but it never worked. He just used to smile at them in his strange way and they'd look confused and go away. It was no good asking him for money anyway, he never had any. His father, Joseph, wasn't all that poor – he was a good carpenter – but Jesus didn't seem interested in money and he used to give all his food away to the really poor children. The nicer rich children used to give him food sometimes: he never asked for anything but he always looked thin and pale and they felt sorry for him. However, he'd eat some of the food, then go and find a sick child or a badly beaten dog to give the rest to.

He was always taking injured animals home. His mother, Mary, used to go wild with all the dogs and cats and hedgehogs and baby birds. And spiders. Jesus had a thing about spiders. If he found a cobweb that had been damaged, he'd look for the spider and take it home, put it in a sheltered corner and watch it while it built a new web. He could watch for hours. His poor mother! Mary gave up the struggle eventually and let him have the whole of the ground floor of their home to look after the animals in his own way. And you know? Their working animals were the strongest and healthiest in the village.

It was when he learned to read that he became really strange. None of the rest of us could read. We had to learn the scriptures, of course, but we used to listen (sort of) to the Rabbi and then recite it back. Sentence by sentence. It was awfully hard, though some of the stories were good – all that eye for an eye stuff. And the wars! Jesus didn't like the gory bits but he had to learn them just the same. Then he'd go off on his own and read and think.

He tried to talk to me about it sometimes. I couldn't get my head round most of it but he used to go on about how we shouldn't try to fight back or steal things or cheat and lie but should love each other. With my legs I couldn't run or fight anyway, but I was a dab hand at cheating and stealing. I couldn't see what was wrong with that when I was young.

I tried to love people. I loved my mum. I didn't have a dad. And I loved my baby sister (mostly). I loved Jesus too, though I wouldn't have called it love in those days. He loved me too, I guess. He would help me and play games with me when my legs were bad. Strangely, they never felt so bad when he was around.

He asked me one day whether I'd like not to be a cripple but I shook my head. It wasn't so bad and it was what I was used to and, besides, if I had good legs I'd have to go out and look after the sheep. Instead, I was allowed to stay with Joseph and carve my models. Joseph was like a dad to me. He used to ask me to encourage Jesus to carve but, you know, Jesus wasn't really interested in making things. He just wanted to read and think and talk. He told the most marvellous stories.

AN AGGRESSIVE SURGEON IN WINDSOR CASTLE

I'm a punctual man, always have been, so when I get a call to say there's an emergency in Windsor Castle I make all haste to complete the morning's business, including the round of golf, and make sure I turn up sharpish, even eating sandwiches in the car on the way to save time.

Imagine my chagrin, therefore, to discover when I arrive that what they wanted was not a real surgeon but a tree doctor. Comes from having the name Birch-Tree and that blasted entry in the telephone directory listing me as Alan Birch-Tree-Surgeon. I've told them about that but they won't change it – say it's what I put on the form.

Well I'm not going to waste my afternoon so I tell them I'm a dab hand at pruning trees and, as it happens, I have my sister's husband Jack's chainsaw in the back of my car. Been there a while now ever since he brought it round to help with the dratted leylandii and forgot to take it home.

So here we go. What do they want doing? Trim that avenue there? OK. Why the emergency? Queen's due tomorrow and the regular man lopped his arm off. Very careless. Ah now, I remember that case. Nasty. Neat job I made of that arm if I may say so myself.

Right, here we go. Out of my way you fellow. You over there get this thing going. You there get some more petrol Where from? How should I know? Siphon it out of the royal coach if you have to.

OK, good swing. My, this thing's powerful. Don't want to damage my fingers; precious asset those. Pow! Wallop! Swing to the right! Swing to the left! Magnificent! Have this tree down to size in no time.

Hmm bit bare on that side now. Good swing to even it up. Good. Not quite what I intended but it'll do. Next!...Next!...Next!...

Get out of my way young fella-me-lad. I don't need your help; just getting into my stride. Magnificent! Next! . . . Next! There that's the lot. Plenty of room for the coach now.

You, put that saw thing back in my car. Which car? Don't be a fool man, I only brought one. Can't drive them all at once.

And you, what do you want? The branches? Take them away. No of course I don't know where they go. Use your common sense, man. Come on, hurry up, haven't got all day. Chop! Chop!

THE DUCK AND THISTLE

'This is not a Brylcreem convention, gentlemen,' Adrian barked, 'I do not want to see the tops of your heads when I am speaking to you. How can you hope to learn what a person is thinking if you are not looking at him?'

'We know what you're thinking,' someone near me murmured.

'Thank you, Mr Payne,' Adrian said, without turning his head. 'I'm sure you do. Born of long experience. And you'd be right. So why do you get it wrong? You should have read these papers before coming here this morning. Now is late. And late is not good enough. I want you here, prepared, in time, *in tempo, in tuno*.'

How many times had I heard those words? Or something similar. To give him his due, Adrian did vary the sarcasms a bit. This was my first day at the police station, on work placement. My long experience of Adrian Lovell was in our local amateur music group. I hadn't known what he did for a living. I always assumed he was a professional conductor. I'd heard him on the radio. I had not known he would be here. It did not surprise me exactly as it seemed to fit him.

He was an excellent conductor, always clear, always with a strong sense of what he wanted us to do and an even stronger conviction that he could get us to do it. '*In tuno*' was a favourite criticism of the violins. Brylcreem references were usually reserved for the elderly basses. Some were not good at reading words and music at the same time. They kept their heads down, not watching the conductor. 'I could put a plastic duck on my head and you wouldn't notice,' was another of his remarks. For that, among other reasons, his most used nickname was The Duck. No-one used it in his hearing, which meant not knowingly in the same building.

I studied Adrian, aka Detective Chief Inspector Lovell. In the music group, I always concentrated on the singing and didn't think about what he looked like. He had fair hair in a conventional short back and sides with a parting, receding at the temples. Mouth turned down at the corners, lips tense, forehead creased in a perpetual frown. Age? I couldn't tell. Marginally taller than me. Five eleven, perhaps. I was five ten. Unlike at choir where he usually wore casual clothes, he was wearing a dark blue suit. It did not make him look smart. The crumpled jacket was unbuttoned, revealing too much of a greyish white shirt. This was also unbuttoned, at the neck. No tie. No belt either and the fastener at the top of the fly of his trousers was not quite clipped in place. I couldn't see his feet. I wondered if he was wearing black or brown shoes. Either would have been in keeping. Or trainers. Or sandals with socks. Whatever he was wearing and however carelessly it was fastened, it would have been a considered choice. He dressed, as someone once said, not to kill but to wound. He wanted to confuse people, to distract them so that they would say or do something unintended.

Unlike most people, who rely on vision for information, Adrian observed with his ears. Confronted with almost one hundred and fifty assorted members of choir and orchestra he could hear what each one of us was doing at any one moment, without apparently looking at us. He could spot a wrong note in a chord anywhere in a score. Woe betide the one who got it wrong, even if there was an error in that poor person's copy. Snarl first, sort out the problem second, apologise never. I was afraid of him but stayed with the choir because the music was so good.

So far I had escaped attention. I wondered if he recognised me. If so he gave no sign. I was an also-ran in the second sopranos, not a brilliant sight-reader but quick at picking up what the others were singing. I was able to get along well enough to avoid personal jibes. I kept my head well up, now. I did not dare glance down at my folder. I had not read it. It had only just been given to me.

It appeared from Adrian's barbed instructions that there had been a murder, probably rape. The victim might have known her attacker. I sensed no sympathy from Adrian. Women got what they deserved, I imagined, if they presented themselves as sexual objects.

My mind wandered while he was haranguing the *gentlemen*. There were quite a few women, I noted. Like my father, Adrian found many women silly and upgraded the non-silly ones to men. In the music group, particularly at music camp where we all had to chip in with chores, there were 'really useful men', 'useful men', 'men', and 'women'. The 'women' were the useless ones who made little effort. Any of these could be male or female.

The room was large, like an old fashioned classroom, with small tables serving as desks in crowded haphazard rows. Once in you could not get out. I was trapped. The air was hot and stuffy, heavy with perfume, aftershave and stale cigarette residue on clothes and hair. His voice faded and I was walking in Oxford Street doing my Christmas shopping, laden with carrier bags, jostled by the crowds. When the lights changed I started to cross a side street but tripped over the kerb. I jerked awake and looked around. There was no sign that anyone had noticed but no doubt Adrian had. I felt sick. I stood up and tried to work out how to get to the nearest window.

'Sit,' Adrian said, as if commanding a dog, without looking at me.

Alpha wolf, I decided. Hunts with the pack. Likes to be in control.

I subsided, muttering. Fatal to mutter but Adrian merely said to the room at large, 'Constable?'

The uniformed person at the end of my skewed row stood, walked the length of the room and opened the farthest window. When she returned she winked at me and pointed out the screw fittings that prevented the other windows from being opened.

'Oh,' I mouthed, 'thank you.'

To keep myself awake I listed the shortcomings of the room. I was training to become an acoustics engineer and had chosen work experience placements where *listening* was important.

We were on the third floor of a 1960s style building, with large badly fitting casement windows. It was noisy from the traffic below. There were no sound absorbing curtains. There was a large white board at one end, badly fitted so it tilted slightly upwards. This would deflect a speaker's voice up, away from the audience. A flip chart was standing in a corner that was probably a dead spot. The flat ceiling was low. It reflected all sound back down, muddling it up if more than one person spoke. Adrian might be able to detect and locate the slightest sound but everyone else was at a disadvantage. They would have difficulty hearing him unless all were quiet.

We were dismissed. When I brushed against Adrian in the crowded doorway I could feel that the suit was fine mohair. The sort of soft lightweight fabric that cries out to be touched. Stroked. Caressed. Did that say something about Adrian?

For the rest of the morning I was scheduled to shadow one of the officers. I found my way to the front desk and asked for Inspector Pamela Smith. I recognised her from the group meeting when I heard her speak sternly to some of the men as we left. She was not tall but was smartly dressed and intimidating. Her manner towards me was not too fierce but I would have to watch my step. She swept me off to her room and said I was to follow her everywhere, even for toilet breaks. I would see how little time she wasted. Watch and listen. Make notes if I wished but not speak. I could save up questions for lunchtime. The time passed uneventfully as I trailed after her and tried to make sense of the bureaucracy.

'So, Miss Ziegler, are you legal?' Adrian's voice close behind me made me jump.

There had been a vote to go to the pub for lunch and I had been volunteered as one of the designated drivers. I was willing enough and had perched up at the solid oak bar with the Inspector and several other officers. They informed me that it would be OK to use first names here, Ma'am in the office, Pam in the pub. I had asked all the questions in my notebook but now found myself alone with Adrian.

'Of course I'm legal,' I retorted. 'I'm told I look like a gypsy but my parents are not illegal immigrants. Neither am I. I was born here. My surname is German. It means brickmaker. Respectable trade. My great grandfather came here from Bavaria.'

Adrian was looking at me oddly. He gestured to the remains of the drink I was holding. It was sparkling water with ice and lemon but it could have been vodka or gin and tonic.

'Oh, that,' I blushed, feeling foolish for misinterpreting. Did he really think I was underage? How embarrassing.

'Oh yes, I'm legal that way too,' I said. 'I'm legal for lots of things, everything I guess where there's an age limit, but,' I added, 'that doesn't necessarily mean I do them.'

The implications of that dawned on me and to cover my confusion I held up my drink, 'This, for instance,' I said, 'is water.'

'Oh and why is that?' Adrian seemed only vaguely interested.

'Cos I'm driving and it's lunch time. Can't hold my liquor at lunch time.'

'Does that mean you can at other times?'

I could feel myself blushing again. I shrugged.

He pointed at my glass.

'Want another?'

He was still looking at me intently. That in itself was unusual and I felt intensely uncomfortable.

I shook my head. 'Must go,' I said and left. The others would have to find their own way back.

My car was blocked by a couple of police vehicles. I was pretty good at wriggling out of tight spots but there was no way I could get out. I went back into the pub, dreading having to face Adrian. He had gone. I found Pam and asked her if she could identify the drivers for me. I let her take over sorting them out.

One of the uniformed constables, fat and balding and in his fifties, leered at me and called out 'Give us a kiss, darlin'.' I smiled at him. He made the mistake of standing up. When I was close enough I kneed him in the groin, tucked my body under his and twisted him onto the floor. He gave a gratifying grunt of pain. Someone cheered. I turned and walked out. I was immensely relieved to find my car had been freed.

I reported to the front desk and waited for the sky to fall. The desk sergeant said I should go straight to the Inspector's office. As I turned to go he winked at me. Conspiratorial or lecherous? Did know? Didn't know?

My knees were weak as I climbed the stairs. The Inspector, back to being Ma'am, looked at me coolly but said nothing. She led me to an inner room, indicated several piles of papers, explained the filing system and asked me to get it sorted.

'We save it up for work experience,' she said with a slight smile. 'Call me if you need anything.' Didn't know?

I became absorbed in the filing and jumped when I turned around to find Adrian close behind me. He made me nervous at the best of times. I looked at his shoes. Soft moccasins. For creeping up on people. He stood close enough for me to feel the soft inviting mohair of his jacket. Too close. The off-white shirt was pale grey silk with a delicate self-coloured pattern. Un-ironed. I could feel the warmth from his body and catch the faint odour of his body sweat. If he was wearing an underarm deodorant, it was un-perfumed. He had a freshly laundered natural smell. I wriggled my toes in my shoes.

'Miss Ziegler,' he said, 'I hear you had an incident in the pub and hurt one of my men.'

I nodded.

'What did he do to upset you?'

'I wasn't upset,' I said.

'You weren't upset and yet you broke a man's collarbone?'

I opened my mouth to speak but nothing came out.

'He's in hospital,' Adrian said.

'How is he? Will he be all right?'

'He'll live. You sound as if you care.'

'I do, I mean, I didn't mean to hurt him, not like that.'

'What exactly did he say to you?'

'Sorry, sir, you'll have to ask him.'

'That's the trouble,' Adrian said, 'I have asked him and he can't think what he did to upset, or offend, you.'

'There were witnesses,' I said, probably a bit peevishly. They had cheered.

'Yes, and they're not talking. Bob says he thinks he smiled and complimented you on your pretty skirt.'

'He didn't mention my skirt, Sir,' I said.

'Ah, I see. Carry on.' He gestured towards the filing and walked off.

I contemplated the remaining mess of papers and settled back down to filing them. The room was warm and airless with a lingering unpleasantness of old coffee and pizza. I could do with some coffee. One good thing - I had not been asked to fetch coffee for everyone else. That was usually the rookie's job. I wondered what would be in store for me. I had made an idiot of myself. Perhaps they would not let me come back. I had been informed most emphatically that placements did not include going on car chases or looking round the forensic labs. Perhaps they'd treat me to a night in the cells.

Not surprisingly, I soon found myself in the superintendent's office. He directed me to stand on a patch of carpet in front of the huge desk, in a position carefully designed to make me feel small and intimidated. Understanding the power game gave me courage but I was still guilty of assaulting a police officer and causing grievous bodily harm.

The Super stood, looked down at me and asked me to describe exactly what had happened.

I did that as fully as I could remember and then he asked,

'Where did you learn such a neat trick, young lady?'

I must have frowned because he laughed and said, 'Am I going to get the same treatment for calling you a young lady?'

'No, Sir.'

'Tell me, then, which do you object to, the "young" or the "lady"?'

'Both together, Sir, it makes me sound as if I'm not worth much.' Which I am not at this particular moment, I thought. I tried to dig myself a hole in the carpet.

'Would you say it was patronising?'

'Yes, Sir. Sorry, Sir.' The carpet refused to budge.

'Don't apologise. Don't ever apologise. You are right. I can see we all still have a lot to learn. *You* must try not to be quite so honest; it's going to get you into trouble. Now then, would you be able to teach your trick to some of my officers?'

'Huh?' What was going on here? 'Yes, Sir, I think so, Sir. I'm only a blue belt but I think I could show them the self-defence moves.'

'Good. And you are not *only* a blue belt and you do not *think* you can teach it. You *are* a blue belt and you *know* you can teach it. Understand?'

I nodded.

'Good.' He seemed about to dismiss me.

'But what about . . .?'

'The incident? The constable was not on duty. That was a private quarrel. He will not bring charges. If he had been fit and alert it would have been you in hospital. Now run along my dear.'

I wondered if he had young daughters and he must have heard the fatherly tone in his voice because he looked up and said, 'That will be all, Miss Ziegler, thank you.'

I was startled awake by a soft footfall behind me.

'Thank you, Thistle, good job,' Adrian said. 'I hope we'll see you tomorrow.'

GOOD NEIGHBOUR

'Good morning,' she said, 'I am collecting on behalf of South Down Hospital for a new scanner.'

The middle-aged man did not reply, but looked at her sourly. Beryl took in his grubby vest that did not cover his pale pot belly and faded jeans worn-through at the knees. She looked around at the untidy garden before trying again.

'I left an envelope here on Monday.'

'You did.'

It was not immediately clear whether he intended this as a question, implying that he had not noticed but would go and look, or criticism for such audacity. Beryl smiled, in what she hoped was a friendly manner. The man turned away and closed the door. Should Beryl wait in case he came back with the envelope? She hesitated a moment but then heard the sounds of dogs, not barking but sniffing and scuffling at the door. Better go.

Beryl backed away, considered whether to take the short cut past the window and thought better of it. She noted the weeds growing up through the cracks in the concrete drive. Some people just didn't know how to look after their property. She didn't like gardening, herself, but that was different; she was a busy woman. She was involved in so many activities for the church she didn't have time for gardening; she relied on her sons to look after that for her. It was their duty.

The letter box of the next house was at the bottom of the door, an awkward stoop, and the stiff bristles of the draft-excluder bruised her fingers. It was unlikely that those thoughtless people would want to contribute. She hastened past. The next house was beautifully kept. The lawn was mown in perfect stripes and had neat borders and nicely trimmed hedges. The double glazing looked new and the panes shone. There was no door bell, but a delightful knocker in the shape of a badger. Nice people here. Beryl knocked and a young woman answered, holding out an envelope.

'Saw you coming. It is for the scanner, isn't it?' Beryl nodded. The young woman patted her belly, 'May be needing that soon, hope you get a good collection.' Beryl smiled and took the envelope. She could feel the shape of a pound coin. Well, every little helps.

Beryl continued trudging up and down the driveways, knocking or ringing, collecting envelopes. Some people in, some out, some smiling, some merely polite, some irritated; some envelopes full, some empty. It was a long street and the hill was steep. Beryl's feet were aching. It was taking her much longer than she'd expected and she'd missed her mid-morning coffee and biscuit. She no longer looked at the house numbers; most houses didn't have a number anyway. Her bag was getting heavy, her shoulders ached and she kept her head down. The task seemed endless, the hill stretched on into the distance before her. Doing good was not easy: the path to righteousness, narrow and steep. Still, she must soldier on.

The next house had an unkempt lawn and weeds sprawling out onto the pavement. Was it worth trying here? Another surly man? Or woman perhaps, not interested in helping the community. The front door was badly in need of painting. Perhaps the occupant was elderly or sick, in need of assistance. Beryl's urge to be a good woman sent her up the path. She rang the bell. There was no sound. Some people! She pressed again. She looked up in distaste as drips fell on her head from dilapidated guttering. There was no reply. She hopped past a broken flower pot and climbed the steps to the next house. Wait a minute, this house was familiar. As she rang the bell and heard its distinctive friendly chime, Beryl looked back at the previous one. She felt dazed and confused. Where was she?

The door opened and a plump woman in a torn house dress, three small children tugging at her skirts, and a plaster cast on one arm, stood there smiling at her.

'Hello, it's Beryl isn't it. It's really nice of you to call. Come on in. Cup of tea? You don't look too well, dear, are you all right? Come on, sit you down. Sorry about the mess. I'll go and put the kettle on.'

Beryl sat down and absently took the teddy bear that one of the children was holding out to her. Her mind whirled. These were her neighbours. The house next door with the leaking guttering – that was her own house. Strange how she'd never noticed what it really looked like. She'd been so busy with good works she'd never visited her neighbours before. She wondered what . . . oh dear, she didn't even know her name - what this woman had done to her arm.

Beryl reflected. She had heard it said that things you despised in other people or that made you angry were just reflections of what you despised or were angry about in yourself. Beryl began to wonder what she was really like, how others saw her.

When her neighbour came back with two mugs of tea, Beryl burst into tears.

'There, there, now, dear. Do you want to tell me what's wrong?'

'Oh dear . . . , I'm sorry, I've forgotten your name, oh, I've been so horrible.'

'I'm Kathy, dear. There, there, you can tell me all about it in a minute. You just drink up your tea, now.'

One of the children bought a box of tissues and held it up for Beryl. She took a tissue and the child climbed up onto her lap and snuggled up against her. Beryl held the child close, smiling up at Kathy through her tears.

LOST ON THE MOON

I've always wanted to go to the Moon and both my parents have promised that I can go when I'm ten. Daddy's a mining engineer and he will take me along with him and he'll take me down the mine. It's a family tradition and my big brother, Richard, went when he was ten but he won't tell me what it's like because he wants it to be a surprise.

Ever since I was tiny I have imagined being high up in the sky lying on the moon, which is just a ball of rock only about two metres across with a hollowed out space where I can lie peering over the edge and looking down at the Earth. I see my baby brother, Jimmy, crawling across the living room trying to find Mummy who's in the kitchen programming the robots for shopping and cooking. Richard is up out in the garden riding his bicycle. It's fun with imagining, especially being able to see down into the living rooms.

Our house is on the coast, built into the cliff, with a great big picture window made of very tough glass on the cliff face so you can see under the water as well as over the top. Fish come right up to the glass and once I saw an enormous purple jellyfish with very long tentacles that Richard says is a Portuguese Man o' War and it's poisonous and can kill you. It's terrific in the storms but it's quite safe.

The garden is huge. Well it's not just our garden, of course, it's shared by all the village, with separate paths for walking and cycling so you can ride very fast. I've seen what the Earth was like when there were still cars and railways and things, before they took down most of the buildings and started living underground, it was very crowded and noisy and dirty and smelly and it must have been horrible.

I like the countryside and the sea. I'm longing for my birthday. What if I got lost on the moon like in my dream one night?

We've landed and Dad and I are climbing into our special Moon suits. It wasn't a long journey, not like in the old days. Mummy programmed the trip; she does all the computer stuff because Dad's hopeless at it. She arranged for a tiny two-person pod to come to the door. It runs over the grass like a hovercraft until it gets to the fast overhead transit and then it hooks up in a line with lots of other pods and whizzes along. That took us to the station and we climbed into the Moon shuttle.

I've been wearing my holo helmet and playing my favourite music most of the time but Dad doesn't like me to wear it and he keeps making me take it off to talk to him and look out of the window. The view over the Earth is beautiful. From the transit you can see for miles and miles and now it's all countryside with just the churches and special historical buildings. Dad started telling me all about the rivers and mountains and the buildings and the people who lived in them but I wasn't listening because I'm too excited. You can't see out of the moon shuttle so Dad lets me keep my holo music on.

The Moon is not two metres across and I've known that a long time now. It's huge and seems the same size as on Earth except that it's just rocks and sand. I practise jumping up and down and I can jump up very high and go a long way with each jump. But I fall over when I land and it takes me a while to learn not to do that but it doesn't hurt much and my moon suit is like a cushion all over me so it's fun to do somersaults and cartwheels.

Dad takes me to the entrance of the mine and introduces me to the other miners and we go down the deep shaft. It's a little bit frightening as it's dark and the cage is very small and I am getting quite worried about getting lost in the tunnels. Sometimes when you dream something is going to happen, it comes true, like when I dreamt I forgot to take my games kit to school and the next day I really forgot. I'm not scared exactly but everyone would think I was silly if I got lost and Daddy would be cross if he had to come looking for me when he was busy so I must be grown up and not get lost. Dad explains that all the tunnels are colour coded with stripes along the floor and I just have to remember which colours to go back. I take extra precautions and have a ball of string in my pocket because I'm colour blind and I might get the colours muddled up. Dad never remembers that. We go down lots of corridors and they get smaller and smaller. Then we have our picnic lunch.

This is fun on the Moon because there is less gravity than on Earth or in the ship which has artificial gravity and if you drop an apple it bounces and you have to jump up to catch it, but you have to be careful not to bump your head on the roof of the tunnel.

Dad then says he has to work for a couple of hours but I can explore. I can go anywhere I like and go back outside if I call for an autocart to take me around. He gets me to recite the colours for getting back to him. I tie the end of my ball of string to a post, just in case, and wander off to see what I can find. I'd like to go back up on the surface of the Moon and explore the craters that we have learned about in school. There is one called Patricia and I'd like to go there because that's my name.

I find the lift shaft and speak into the intercom and give the number Daddy told me and go up to the surface. The sun is very bright. There is not much string left and I tie the end near the entrance and speak into the intercom again and climb into the little robot autocart when it comes and tell it to take me to a crater. It shows me a map on the monitor and I point to the one called Patricia. It says it's only five kilometres across so I will be able to walk that easily. It'll be fun to tell the others that I walked all the way across a crater. None of my friends has been on the moon yet.

I'm not worried about getting lost out here as the autocart will look after me and I've got plenty of air and drinks and sandwiches. I know all about checking for air and things because Mummy and Daddy have taken me and Richard diving in the sea and I have my Padi scuba diving certificate.

We get to the Patricia crater and I jump out of the cart and run across, jumping up high all the way across and then I find a cave. The autocart has followed along with me and I tell it to wait outside because it's too big to go into the cave and if I'm not back in half an hour it must signal to Daddy and get someone to find me. It would be serious to get lost here. I haven't got any more string but I'll count how many right and left turns I take.

The cave is big at first but then it gets smaller but I can still stand up and actually there aren't any turns and the tunnel goes further and further into the mountain and my helmet torch lights up in front of me and I can see quite well. I keep checking my air and it's OK. It's a boring tunnel and there's nothing to look at and I'm beginning to get hungry and decide I must go back to the autocart when suddenly I trip over something and fall down. I roll over and over and my light goes out and I can't feel where I'm going but I'm doing a sort of roly poly down a long slope. Then I hit something and stop. I don't think I'm hurt or anything and I get up on my hands and knees and start to crawl about to see if I can feel my way to the slope.

My foot hits something soft. I turn around and feel what it is and there is a person there all crumpled up. I find its head and feel for the helmet lamp and it lights up. It's a girl about my age. I check her air and it has nearly run out so I hook her up to my supply and hope there will be enough to get us both back to the cart. She isn't badly hurt and soon she wakes up and can talk to me. Her name is Ann and her aunty works in the mine and she came exploring just like me but she can't remember where she left her autocart and she fell over and must have punctured her air supply. It was very lucky I came along in time to save her. As I didn't see any other autocart we think she must have come in a different way.

There are two steep slopes leading down into the pit where we have fallen and we don't know which is mine and which is Ann's. We do eeny meeny miney mo and take one of the slopes. It's not that difficult to climb, except that Ann keeps turning away from me so I can't see and I have to keep asking her to turn round, and we scramble back up to a tunnel. I can't tell if it's mine or not and Ann doesn't recognise anything either. Then I know it must be Ann's as it branches off ahead of us. I get a bit panicky because there's not much air left and we don't know where we are but Ann looks up at the roof and finds a mark scratched into the softer rock. She's a scout just like me and she has left a trail. We follow her marks back to the outside and find her autocart and send a signal to Daddy who tells us Ann's aunty was only just beginning to get worried about Ann. When we get back to the mine everyone is very pleased to see us.

SISTERS

Lift up the phone! Now!
Or I will come and kill you.
I'll avenge our mum,
whom you all dare to neglect
in your dire complacency.

Come back dear sister,
from your deep painful sorrow,
from your wild madness.
We share your love and concern,
our mum will not die alone.

Author's Note: Like *Sail with Me*, this is a Somonka, a form of Japanese love poem which is composed of two tankas or five line poems with syllable counts 5-7-5-7-7. In this case, the first tanka is a statement of grief that has come out as hate and anger. The second is the response.

THE YELLOW HAT

It was quiet in the church and felt as if the rest of the town had disappeared. Timothy saw the woman in the yellow hat kneel and pretend to close her eyes. He could see she wasn't really praying - she was watching the people around her to see when it would be the right time to sit up again. He wondered why she bothered to pretend. If Timothy didn't feel like praying, he didn't pretend. God would know when he was ready to pray and He wouldn't mind waiting a bit, and it was silly to pretend since God could tell. God wouldn't mind though. He would probably smile and find a way to help.

At the end of the service, Timothy saw the woman pretend to pray again and then get up and leave the church. His mother was busy giving out the coffee so Timothy fetched the slice of wholemeal bread from her bag and followed the woman out. He saw her shake hands with the vicar and say what a lovely service it was.

When the vicar shook hands with Timothy, Timothy did not say what a lovely service it had been. He didn't say what a long service it had been, either. He didn't say anything and he tried not to mind, and to smile, when the vicar said how much he had grown. He didn't think he could have grown much since last week.

And then it happened. A pigeon flew down from one of the windows and messed all over the yellow hat. The woman didn't notice but some big children did and they laughed. Timothy wondered who this woman was who came to church on her own and didn't know how to pray. He ran after her and stood in front of her with his arm up like a policeman so that she stopped.

'Come with me,' he said, 'and I'll show you where to wash it.' He pointed to her hat. She took off her hat and looked at it. She didn't say anything but she made a face.

'Over here,' Timothy said and led her back into the church. He took her to the secret place with the sink and pulled aside the curtain. He found her a cloth and some soap. It was yellow soap, shaped like a lemon. He watched the woman wash her yellow hat with the yellow soap. The soap smelled of lemon and made Timothy think of his Nan.

His mother popped her head round the curtain.

'Everything under control, Timmy?'

He nodded.

'Are you new here?' His mother asked the woman with the yellow hat.

Everything *was* under control *now*. Timothy went outside to look for the pair of ducks that had made their nest in a patch of grass behind the church where they were sheltered from the passers-by and the busy town centre traffic.

SAIL WITH ME

Sail with me again
to distant lands and people,
across the ocean.
Dive with me among corals.
Lie with me under the stars.

I cannot return
to your slim fragile prison.
The sea is too deep,
darkness and storms frighten me,
and who will tend my garden?

Author's Note: This is a Somonka, a form of Japanese poem which is composed of two tankas or five line poems with syllable counts 5-7-5-7-7. The first tanka is a statement of love. The second is the response.

CRISS-CROSS

My proportions feel different, my feet are too far down the bed and when I touch my leg it's more like Christopher's rough hairy skin than my own smooth thigh. Wow! Magic!

It feels right. I always wanted to be the boy, the firstborn twin. So, I am Christopher now; not Tina any more. Tina must be dead. The plane must have crashed.

'Hello,' I call out in my brother's rich baritone, 'hello, it's me, Christopher. Can you hear me?'

I explore with my hands in the darkness. Christopher is a big man. I wonder about Christopher's girlfriends. I remember Moira.

In the morning, I find I am in the farmhouse on Dartmoor where Iain and I had our honeymoon. The farmer rescued me from the crash. Walking is not easy. I'll need to adjust to being six foot two. Using the loo is fun.

I find a bicycle. Cycling is strange. At first I can't work out how to get my leg over the saddle. I scoot awkwardly then suddenly I'm riding furiously. Approaching a steep downward drop, I can't slow down. I scream as I had as a little girl when Christopher had put me on his crossbar.

It's dark and raining hard, I catch a bus into Plymouth, head for the Barbican, and find a favourite pub, from when Christopher and I were underage.

'Brown and mild, please.'

'Leastways 'tis not blunkin,' the bartender says, gesturing at the rain. 'Vurriner ere?'

I laugh at the dialect so familiar from my childhood. Foreigner? I suppose so in a way. I agree that it's a good thing it isn't snowing.

I meet a lesbian couple, Lyn and Pauline, and their gay friends, David and Mark. They can tell at once, they say, that I'm not 'straight'. I can't explain. They decide they must help me sort out my sexuality.

They take me dancing. I love the feel of the women in my arms. Could be right for me, perhaps. Not for them. David teaches me to 'wine' like a Trinidadian: all pelvis. Mark propositions me; openly, with no preliminary games or pretexts. Coyly, I accept. He is lovely. Solicitous like Iain. Smells different though. Distinctive. His skin is smooth dark chocolate. When I let go of my inhibitions I love the feel of his hard muscles, the vigour, the turn-taking.

I find a card in Christopher's flying jacket with Moira's address. When she opens the door she is wearing the same tight short black dress she'd worn at our twenty-first party and she doesn't look much older, just glamorous and sexy.

'Chrissy, darling, How wonderful to see you. Ooh! You're all wet. Get your kit your kit off! Mmm, nice. It's been a long time, Gorgeous.'

I let Moira take charge and reach out hesitantly to touch her breasts when she conveniently places them within easy reach. I have always been embarrassed by breasts but this is wonderful. Wonderful. I smother my face in her generous bosom. No wonder men go so wild. As we make love I try to imagine what I would have liked when I was Tina, that Iain didn't do.

I hear the plaintive long drawn out whistle of a distant train. It is time, I decide, to go and see Iain so I take a train to London to find him and the twins.

Miraculously, in Hamley's, in the model railway department – Iain's favourite – there they are. It feels strange. We shake hands politely.

'You could come back to Thame with us,' Iain says. 'I could do with some adult company. I miss Tina dreadfully.'

It is fantastic being home. Nothing has changed. Even the sweet peas on the table are the same. I keep having to remind myself that

I am Christopher. Brother-in-law. Uncle. Not Tina, wife and mother. I have so much energy. I help Iain mend the dangerously broken crazy paving in the front garden. I seal the leaky guttering. I mow the lawn. I do all those things Tina avoided.

I grow very fond of them. It is so different being uncle instead of mother. I am no longer tired and depressed and I love playing games. The twins respond to me as they do to Iain, enthusiastically and energetically, not whiningly and complainingly as they had done when I was Tina.

We go to St Neot in Cornwall for a few days. Iain had asked for Tina's ashes to be buried in St Neot graveyard, next to Jane, our mother, who died giving birth to me, and he wants to take Sula and Petra to visit the graves. Tina's ashes. My ashes. We crush rose petals so that their perfume is released and scatter them on both the graves and share tears for Jane and Tina.

We build a studio and I start to paint in oils, big paintings using a palette knife, bold, loose and free. The paintings are abstract but tell stories of death and rebirth.

I want to dance. I suggest to Iain that we should go to classes together and hint that we might be able to pick up some girls. Iain is dubious and insists that he wants to stay faithful to Tina, but he agrees to come with me, and that is how I meet Debbie.

Sex with Debbie is conservative, but intensely sweet. I go softly, asking permission with my touch, inviting her to touch and explore. Mark and Moira had each talked all the time – in blunt crude language – but I don't want to talk; I don't want to disturb the wordless magic with words. I *paint* her.

As soon as we can arrange it, we all go down to Hamble for the weekend to look at the yacht that Iain bought after Tina died. When I was Tina I hated the idea of going sailing or learning to swim.

Swimming is a problem: Iain knows that Christopher used to be a champion so I can hardly confess that I can't swim.

Eventually I can't put it off any longer. Perhaps my body can swim without me interfering, like with the bicycle, or maybe I can learn for myself. I try, and soon, to my amazement, I can do a few strokes with me in control. OK. Takes a bit of practice. Iain and the twins join me and I proudly show them what I can do, forgetting for the moment that I am not Tina. The twins fall about laughing.

'Oh, Uncle Chris, you are such a good actor,' Petra says, 'you look just like a beginner. Come on, I'll show you how to do it properly.' Under her expert tuition, I 'pretend' to learn to swim.

Debbie, like Tina, is frightened of the water.

'Tina could have learned, if only she'd tried,' I say.

'Tina?' Debbie sounds faintly scornful. 'You're always telling me what a wimp your sister was. You didn't like your sister much, did you?'

What? Christopher had loved me but it was true, I had not loved myself.

'Tina found having children so difficult you see,' I say to Debbie. 'She didn't know how to fit them in with her painting so she gave up painting and then resented the twins, I think. But she wasn't painting anyway, she felt blocked, too many deaths, too many house moves, she was too restricted by marriage and everyone's expectations of her as a wife and mother. She needed a wife, I think.'

I had never said that to anyone. Didn't actually know it myself until then.

Debbie groans, 'All career women need a wife-person but unfortunately not many men want to take that role. What about us, Chris? Do you like me?'

'Ah Debbie, of course I do. I love you. You are very talented with your cello. You know where you're going and you're prepared to work hard to get there.'

'Do you love me enough to be my wife-person? While I follow my career?'

I have no answer to that. I was no good at being a wife.

'I can see you are not so sure about that. Typical man! And you, Chris, do you see yourself as talented?'

'I'm working on it,' I say.

One day after a summer family picnic, Debbie is very quiet.

'You're gay aren't you,' she says abruptly. 'I've seen the way you look at Iain. He doesn't notice, but I do. I wish you looked at me like that.'

I am startled. My wishful thinking about her crumbles. We are good friends but I am not the man she thinks I am. I can't possibly explain. Had I been looking at Iain? What did I feel for him? I had once, long ago it seems, loved him – emotionally and sexually. I love him now, as brother-in-law, and I love our children and I want to go on living with them.

'I'm sorry, Debbie,' I say.

Then comes the long awaited weekend when we are ready to sail across to France. Great excitement.

What do I feel for Iain? Suddenly I want him. Was Debbie right? Am I gay? Would this be a possible future for us? Surely not. Iain could never want that and how would we ever explain to Petra and Sula? The world might now accommodate many different family arrangements but as a man I can't begin to contemplate making love to Iain. No, it doesn't bear thinking about. But I want him.

We cross the Channel and spend a few days exploring the coast of France. I love every minute of it. As the wind rises and the sea becomes choppy, Iain and I work well as a team, not needing to talk. The weather worsens and we have to fight to keep the boat on course and clear of the rocks. I have never felt so close to Iain, or so far apart. Iain is not gay. I can't let him know how I feel about him. I'll have to think of something. In the meantime the yacht takes all our energy as Iain and I pit our wits and our brawn against the elements.

At last, the weather calms. We relax and open cans of beer. It is a golden moment.

It hits me that it is not Christopher who is in love with him. The parts that melt in me, when he comes near enough for me to smell his familiar tangy sweat, belong to Tina. I'd thought that Tina had gone, but that isn't true.

I want to be Iain's wife as I had been before, not the brother of his dead wife and a good friend. I want to be the mother of my children, not their uncle.

Dense fog comes down suddenly, Iain checks the lights and I go to fetch the air horn and give a good few ear shattering blasts.

Iain wrenches the wheel hard over and shouts, 'Watch out! Hold on!'

A tanker has loomed up out of the fog and is about to run us down. I yell to the girls to go below. As they move, the yacht tips violently and they are thrown out of the cockpit and over the side into the sea.

I dive in. I have no chance of finding the girls in the fog. No-one has any chance of finding them. Or me.

I am cold. I hear seagulls.

I can hear the rustle of sheets. I feel strong arms lifting me. I am warm, drowsy, comfortable.

'Hello, Tina' I hear my brother's voice, 'hello, it's me, Christopher, can you hear me?'

I start to cry that I am Christopher and Tina is dead, that the twins have drowned and that Iain is probably lost too. But Iain is with me, smiling, hugging me, kissing me. Christopher too, and Sula and Petra. There is a jar of sweet peas on the hospital bedside table and a scattering of dried rose petals.

WHICH DIAGNOSIS?
or
CLARITY BEGINS AT HOME

If my house strikes you as dirty
Pity me
For I am lonely and depressed
And don't know what to do

If my house strikes you as clean
Pity me
For I am lonely and depressed
And don't know what else to do

If my house strikes you as dirty
Envy me
For I am happy and fulfilled
And have other things to do

If my house strikes you as clean
Envy me
For I am happy and fulfilled
And have someone in to 'do'.

If my house strikes you as dirty
Rouse me
For I am dull and slow
And can't get into a routine

If my house strikes you as clean
Rouse me
For I am dull and slow
And can't get out of my routine

If my house strikes you as dirty
Soothe me
For I am tense and agitated
Running round in useless circles

If my house strikes you as clean
Soothe me
For I am tense and agitated
Running round in needless circles

If my home strikes you as friendly
Come on in.

Lightning Source UK Ltd.
Milton Keynes UK
UKHW020838110721
386955UK00009B/376